He was *their* son.

And Ty was entranced with him.

He'd never really watched a baby's antics before, and he was mesmerized—with more than Jordan. There was such a look of devotion on Marissa's face. Her eyes sparkling with the joys of motherhood, she was absolutely beautiful. Beautiful in a way he hadn't recognized before.

"I've never held a baby," he admitted to her.

Her lips quirked up. "They're just as squiggly as a baby calf."

That analogy brought an unexpected chuckle from him. "Okay." He'd held on to baby calves before.

Marissa was close enough that he caught the scent of her. Oh, how he remembered that scent. That night he'd made love to her, her hair had smelled like flowers, and that's the scent he caught now. It triggered a response in his body that was totally inappropriate. He willed himself to block off any attraction to her. To focus on Jordan.

He slid his large hands under Jordan's tiny arms and lifted him from Marissa's hold. His little boy was solid and warm.

His little boy.

Ty's chest constricted and his throat tightened. Just what in the blue blazes was happening to him?

* * *

THE MOMMY CLUB:
It's about caring, family...and love.

Dear Reader,

A baby changes everything!

When our son was born, the world became brand-new. Even though he's grown, the world is new again when we see him. Parents never forget the memories they hold in their hearts. They never forget the first smile, the first step, the first day at school, the first day their child starts a job. A parent's heart can hold all their child's years in a flash of joyful remembrance.

When my hero—rodeo cowboy Ty Conroy—learns he has a son, his life changes dramatically. He thought he lost everything in a bull riding accident, only to find "everything" in his son...and the child's mother. Marissa and Ty must overcome their pasts to find their future. Love for their son unites them and leads them to a true understanding of giving and receiving love. I hope you enjoy their romantic journey as they find their happily-ever-after.

I look forward to interacting with readers. My website, karenrosesmith.com, is the portal to my latest news, releases and social media feeds. For day-to-day chatting, search on Facebook for KarenRoseSmithBooks. Follow me on Twitter, @KarenRoseSmith. I hope each and every one of my books brings you reading pleasure.

Karen Rose Smith

The Cowboy's Secret Baby

Karen Rose Smith

HARLEQUIN® SPECIAL EDITION®

Recycling programs
for this product may
not exist in your area.

ISBN-13: 978-0-373-65904-3

The Cowboy's Secret Baby

Copyright © 2015 by Karen Rose Smith

This edition published by arrangement with Harlequin Books S.A.

For questions and comments about the quality of this book, please contact us at CustomerService@Harlequin.com.

Printed in U.S.A.

www.Harlequin.com

USA TODAY bestselling author **Karen Rose Smith**'s 87th novel will be released in 2015. Her passion is caring for her four rescued cats, and her hobbies are gardening, cooking and photography. An only child, Karen delved into books at an early age. Even though she escaped into story worlds, she had many cousins around her on weekends. Families are a strong theme in her novels. Find out more about Karen at karenrosesmith.com.

Books by Karen Rose Smith

Harlequin Special Edition

The Mommy Club

A Match Made by Baby
Wanted: A Real Family

Reunion Brides

Riley's Baby Boy
The CEO'S Unexpected Proposal
Once Upon a Groom
His Daughter...Their Child

Montana Mavericks: Rust Creek Cowboys

Marrying Dr. Maverick

The Baby Experts

Twins Under His Tree
The Texan's Happily-Ever-After
The Texas Billionaire's Baby
Baby by Surprise
The Midwife's Glass Slipper
Lullaby for Two

Montana Mavericks: The Texans are Coming!

His Country Cinderella

Montana Mavericks: Thunder Canyon Cowboys

From Doctor...to Daddy

Visit the Author Profile page at Harlequin.com for more titles.

To my son...
who has always made everything brand-new.

Chapter One

Marissa Lopez's heart began beating faster. Her stomach seemed to turn upside down. Oh, no. That couldn't be Ty Conroy over there, could it?

She'd stopped in at the physical therapy center to talk to her friend, Sara Cramer. On her lunch hour, she didn't have a whole lot of time. But she needed Sara's advice.

However, now—

"What's wrong?" Sara asked. "You suddenly went pale."

Marissa pointed her chin toward the other side of the room, where one of the physical therapists was sitting in a chair across from Ty.

Ty.

The father of her baby. Ty. The father of her baby who didn't *know* he was the father of her baby.

Sara looked in the direction Marissa had indicated. "Do you know him?" she asked.

Sara wasn't from Fawn Grove. She didn't recognize the boy who had made good in the rodeo riding circuit. She didn't know the bull rider who Marissa had spent a night with. A mistaken, foolish night.

Although she could never even think about her life without her son, Jordan. Not for a moment.

Sara was one of the few people who knew the name of her baby's father.

"That's Ty Conroy," Marissa answered in a shaky voice.

Sara's eyes went wide. "Are you serious? What are you going to do?" She knew Marissa had never expected Ty Conroy to return to Fawn Grove, California.

"Do you know why he's here?" Marissa asked, edging toward the door.

Sara shook her head. "I don't work with him. Even if I did, I couldn't tell you—patient privacy and all that."

Marissa couldn't help but take another glance at Ty, who was now minus his cowboy hat and boots. His hand was on his knee and she spotted a cane leaning against the table. Just what had happened?

She was definitely out of that bull riding loop. Her job at Jase Cramer's winery, Jordan and her volunteer work with The Mommy Club, an organization that helped parents in need, captured all of her attention and energy. She rarely even watched the news or any TV for that matter, except for SpongeBob and The Disney Channel. Sara was the same. They were both busy women.

Her glance at Ty lingered a little bit too long. The physical therapist moved away from him and Ty's gaze zeroed right in on hers.

Oh, no! she thought again.

Though she told herself to look away, her eyes took him in. Two years hadn't made much difference in her appearance, nor had they made much difference in his, though there were more lines around his eyes now.

Where before his expression had been pensive, now he broke into a grin and motioned her over.

She groaned.

"How are you going to play this?" Sara asked, clearly worried for her.

"I don't know," Marissa murmured. "I need some time to think about it."

"You can run out of here," Sara suggested.

"Running never helped anything. I'll just have to figure this out as I go."

Ty motioned to her again. She walked across the room, every step filling her with anxiety, every inch closer to him making her pulse race faster. They'd definitely had chemistry that night, and she could feel it now, even this far away from him.

He looked glad to see her and that made her feel even worse.

By the time she reached him, he was on his feet. Even without his boots, he was over six feet tall, and those broad shoulders—

In a snap-button shirt, with the collar open and his sleeves rolled up, he looked good enough to…to…hug. But she wasn't about to do that.

He was still smiling.

Before he could say a word, she blurted out, "What are you doing here?" Once the question was out, she couldn't take it back. Besides, she had to know.

"I've been back about two months," he said, not really answering her question.

She motioned to the physical therapy room. "But what are you doing *here*?"

He looked down at his left leg and grimaced. "I guess the latest gossip hasn't reached you."

Fawn Grove was a small town, and if you kept your ear to the ground, and the coffee shop, and the family diner, and the feed store, rumors floated all over the place. But she didn't get to any of those places. Besides, only Sara and their friend Kaitlyn knew she'd had a fling with Ty. So why would anybody tell her anything about him?

"So let's bypass the gossip and get to the truth," she suggested.

His Stetson was on a chair beside the table where he'd sat. He studied it for a moment, then raised his gaze to hers. "My rodeo days are over. A bull got the best of me, and I had to have a knee replacement."

Wow! She hadn't been expecting that.

"When did it happen?"

"About four and a half months ago. I had surgery in Houston, and I did rehab there. But I've come back to the Cozy C to help out my uncle, to get plans going that we started when I was in Houston. The doc in Texas thought it was a good idea if I continued physical therapy here, considering I wanted to be back in the saddle sooner rather than later."

"You'll be able to ride again?" she asked, knowing how much it meant to him.

"I am riding. Horses, not bulls." His tone was wry and she suspected there were a lot of feelings behind it. However he didn't express them.

"I did hear your uncle's having a tough time of it." Jase Cramer, Sara's husband, had mentioned he was thinking about buying the Cozy C property if it ever went up for sale. He'd mentioned Eli Conroy was having a problem paying his taxes. She'd briefly thought of Ty when she'd heard that, but she'd never imagined he'd be back here.

"Yeah, Uncle Eli has had it rough. He was finally honest with me about it after this happened. But I won my best purse ever the night that bull did me in. So Uncle Eli and I are going to turn the Cozy C into a vacation ranch."

Marissa supposed that was one solution. That would take an awful lot of money, and one huge overhaul. Which meant Ty was going to stay around…

She had to get out of here. She couldn't make chitchat with him. She didn't want him to find out anything she didn't want him to know, at least not yet. Though she understood in her soul that the day was coming when she'd have to tell him about Jordan.

She checked her watch. "I'm on my lunch hour and I have to get back to work. It was great to see you. Good luck with your uncle's ranch."

And before Ty could say another word, could even utter a goodbye, she turned and fled.

Ty stared after Marissa Lopez, totally baffled by what had just happened. When their gazes had connected across the room, he'd seen the same sparks there now that he'd seen when they'd attended the wedding of friends together two years ago. They'd known each other years before that. They'd gone to the same high school, known some of the same kids, though he'd been two years older than Marissa and had stayed away from her. No easy feat, because she'd been a beauty even back then.

Automatically his thoughts returned to the wedding they'd attended in Sacramento. He'd known the groom and she'd known the bride. At the reception, they'd hooked up. Then they'd gone back to his motel room.

That had been a night that had been hard to put out of his memory. That had been a night he'd even thought about the day the bull had ended his career. Thinking about Marissa had helped him deal with the pain. He had to admit he'd intended to look her up again eventually—when he was whole once more, when this PT was all done with, when the Cozy C was an amazing success. He didn't know why all that had been important, but it had been.

Seeing her today...

His gaze still on her as she headed toward the door, he watched the receptionist stop her. He listened, without being concerned at all about eavesdropping.

The blonde at the reception desk asked, "Are you going to be helping with The Mommy Club food drive for Thanksgiving?"

Casting a quick glance his way, Marissa turned her back to him, nodded and then murmured something in reply.

Then she was gone.

Just like she'd been gone the morning after their night of passion.

He'd awakened as she'd dressed, but he'd known they really hadn't had anything to say. He was going out on the circuit again. She would be staying in Fawn Grove. He didn't know when he'd be back. So he'd let her leave without a word.

And that had been that.

But the receptionist's question stuck with him.

The Mommy Club? What did Marissa have to do with *that*? Every once in a while he checked in on Fawn Grove's Chamber of Commerce's Facebook page, just to see what events were going on, what was happening in the town he'd grown up in. He vaguely remembered seeing postings about The Mommy Club.

As soon as he got back to the ranch, he'd have to check it out.

As Ty opened the newly painted white wooden screen door and stepped into the Cozy C's renovated kitchen, he was barely mindful of the smell of new paint and coffee. Yet he couldn't miss the sight of his uncle Eli sitting at the oak pedestal table nursing a mug of a dark brew.

"You're leaning on that cane pretty heavy. Tough workout?" his uncle asked.

If it were up to Ty, the cane would be tossed into the recycle bin. He rarely used it now, though his physical therapist wanted him to. But after today's exercises, he needed to ice the muscles around his knee before getting along with his day.

"No tougher than any other," he assured his uncle, leaving the cane by the door and hanging his Stetson on the hat hook. There were four of them there now, for any of the dude ranch's guests who came to visit the main house's kitchen.

"Still smells like paint in here," his uncle grumbled.

"You wanted to keep the wooden door. It needed a facelift."

"And that stainless-steel stove and refrigerator make

me want to close my eyes when I come in here in the morning. It's so damn bright."

That was an exaggeration if Ty ever heard one, but he could tell his uncle was in a complaining mood.

"You like the new touch faucet, though, don't you?"

His uncle glanced at it and scowled. "I liked that old white porcelain sink just fine. And in my day, a spigot for hot and a spigot for cold was all I needed. Now we've got that fancy sprayer and a filtered water tap." Eli shook his head.

"Any complaints about the new guest cabins?" Ty asked, amused by his uncle's rant.

"If somebody wants to stay here, they should be happy with the bunkhouse," Eli muttered.

"You can't expect a family to stay in a bunkhouse, even if we did give it an overhaul and a more refined look. Single guys who come for the ranch experience can bunk with the hands there. But what if we get a couple who wants to explore the area on horseback for their honeymoon?"

"So you want to provide a love nest?" Eli sounded aghast at that thought.

"I want to provide a cozy cabin where they'll be happy so they spread the word to their friends and we get even more guests. Instead of all these changes, would you have rather sold the Cozy C?"

They'd had the conversation many times since Eli had confessed the state of the ranch while Ty was still in Houston. Ty supposed his uncle hadn't wanted him to return and be shocked by what he found. And Ty would have been. When he returned two months ago, the place had been sorely run-down. The tax collector had been on Eli's doorstep for the past year. With his bull riding winnings tucked into a bank account, Ty had been able to think, plan and move fast—from his rehab facility in Houston. He and his uncle had spent long sleepless nights over this decision before renovations started, but there really had been no other choice but to turn the Cozy C into an income-generating ranch.

Now Eli took a long swig of coffee, then set down his mug with a thump. "I still don't like the idea of using all your winnings for this. You could have had a sweet retirement fund."

"That's a long way off."

At twenty-nine, Ty had plenty of years to worry about retirement. If they could make a success of the Cozy C, he and his uncle would both be set.

"This place is going to be great, Unc. You'll see."

Eli pushed his chair back, stood, and went to the new sink. "All I see is you working day and night when you should still be recuperating."

"I'm done recuperating. Haven't you noticed?"

Eli turned and looked him in the eye. "I don't know if you've ever started."

Ty wasn't even going to ask what *that* meant, though his uncle was probably referring to his childhood, not just the bull riding accident. Ty had spent the first few years of his life in Texas. Vague memories that had to do with dust and heat and hills sometimes shadowed his dreams. His dad had ridden the circuit and his mom, well, she'd gotten tired of the whole thing—the dust, the heat, as well as being alone and taking care of a child all by herself. One weekend, when his dad had come home between rodeos, she'd announced she was leaving. Not only leaving, but she was leaving Ty with his dad.

His father hadn't had a clue how to take care of a

four-year-old, so he'd called his brother Eli. In no time, the two had moved to Fawn Grove, California, and the Cozy C. Once they had, his dad had gone on the circuit again. He'd been killed by an ornery bull a few years later. Maybe Ty had gone into bull riding to prove he wouldn't have the same fate.

No, not the same. A different one.

Needing to change the topic of conversation, Ty went to the coffeepot and filled his own mug. Standing there as casually as he could, he said offhandedly, "I ran into Marissa Lopez in town."

"That gal who turned your head when you were in high school?"

"She didn't turn my head. She was two years younger and—"

Eli cut in and waved his hand. "Never no mind. Just stay away from her. She had a baby with no dad in sight. You don't want to get tangled up in that kind of complication."

She'd had a *baby*? That's why she was involved in The Mommy Club.

"How old's her baby?" Ty asked.

"A year, maybe a couple of months more. It's not like I keep track of everybody in town."

A year? Fourteen months? His heart pounded in his ears.

His uncle acted as if he didn't keep track, but Eli often drove into the diner for breakfast, and he and his cohorts gossiped as much as any women's group. They knew the comings and goings. They knew the old-time residents. They knew who was new. They just knew.

Making quick calculations in his head, Ty didn't like what he came up with. *If* her baby was a couple of months over a year old, and it took nine months to have a baby…

That would put the night of conception right about when he and Marissa had hooked up after the wedding.

He hoped he was totally mistaken. The thing was, he had to find out…and soon.

Ty didn't like the looks of the apartment building at all. It was shabby, like the landlord could care less about it. Its pale yellow stucco had seen too much sun. The pavement was cracked under Ty's boots as he walked around the back of the building to the apartments on that side. Checking the address on his phone again, he saw that Marissa's apartment was the middle one, on the second floor. He mounted the stairs and the finish of the railing came off like powder on his hand. Sure, maybe he'd stay in a place like this on a long rodeo stint, but it was no place for a mother and a child. He imagined Marissa was living here because she could afford the rent. Still…

Just where did Marissa work? Did she make enough money to support her and her baby? Was there a guy in the picture now?

He remembered again the wedding they'd attended in nearby Sacramento. They'd been on opposite sides of the aisle in the church, he on the groom's side and she on the bride's. But he'd ended up behind her in the receiving line and they'd taken seats at the same table at the dinner. They'd talked some, laughed at high school escapades they'd remembered. They'd shared the bride and groom's happiness as the couple had exchanged pieces of cake and then danced. That's when the real night had started for him and Marissa. He'd asked her to dance.

That dance…

It had started the rest of the night.

At the top of the stairs, he stood at her door, which was decorated with a wreath of autumn leaves, nuts and gourds, not knowing exactly the right way to handle this. Maybe there was no *right* way.

He pressed the doorbell, but when he didn't hear it ring, he knocked. It was after six. She should be home having dinner, taking care of her baby.

When she opened the door, he saw that she'd changed from the beige slacks and cream shirt into worn jeans and a T-shirt that proclaimed JORDAN'S MOMMY.

So she had a son, and his name was Jordan.

She looked horrified when she saw him glancing down at her T-shirt. Her face went pale. But he had to give her credit. After a deep breath, another second and a lifetime later, she produced a smile.

"Hi, Ty. I didn't think I'd see you so soon. What brings you here?"

She was holding the door three-quarters of the way closed behind her, but he could hear sounds coming from inside the apartment. They sounded like baby squeals.

He motioned behind her. "Can I come in?"

She glanced over her shoulder. "It's not a good time."

"When would be a good time?" he asked in a compromising tone.

"I don't know. I'm fixing supper, and then I have work to do. My to-do list is pretty full this week."

No matter what she did or said, he was determined to have a talk with her.

"Invite me in, Marissa, for old time's sake. I won't stay long."

With another glance over her shoulder, she gave a huge sigh, opened the door and motioned him in.

He couldn't read the expression on her face. Was it dread, nervousness, regret? He'd love to know what was going on in her head.

He walked in and saw the baby right away. On the rodeo circuit Ty had talked with kids and horsed around with them. He liked their innocence and naïveté and optimistic outlook on life. They made him laugh. But he'd never been around *babies*.

This little fellow was seated in a high chair, playing with little round cereal pieces on his tray. Ty barely noticed the yellow-and-white kitchen curtains, the skillet simmering on the stove with what looked like barbecued beef. The smell wafted through the kitchen but it didn't even make his stomach growl. He couldn't take his eyes off the little boy.

"My uncle told me you're unmarried and you have a baby."

Marissa kept silent.

"How old is he?"

As if Jordan wanted to answer for himself, he pounded his tiny fist on the plastic tray, squealed and gave a lopsided toothy grin to Ty. Ty's heart turned over in his chest.

"He's fourteen months old," Marissa said.

Ty's gaze swung to hers. He could see she was trying hard to hold it together, to act as if nothing were the matter, acting as if that hadn't been the most important question in the world.

"We used protection," he said matter-of-factly.

"Not in the middle of the night," she reminded him softly.

How could he have forgotten *that*? How could he have forgotten they'd reached for each other, half-asleep, come together as if they'd been lovers for years and rocked the bed as if lightning was striking all over again?

"He's mine."

She only hesitated a moment, and then he saw what he'd sensed about her from the very beginning—from the time they were in high school. She was honest and wouldn't lie.

"Yes, he's yours. His name is Jordan."

As if he was drawn by a very powerful magnet, he crossed to the child and stared down at him, trying to let the implications of it all wash over him. The little boy was pounding on his tray again, gleefully burbling, kicking his legs. He had Ty's brown hair, a much lighter shade than Marissa's. But the baby had Marissa's dark brown eyes, sparkling and shiny with new life and expectant hope.

Suddenly the gravity of what was happening hit Ty in the solar plexus. He swiveled on his boots, faced her and said, "You should have told me."

She looked dumbstruck for a second.

He held up his hand, knowing they both needed to take a few deep breaths. "I need some air. I'm going for a walk, but I'll be back. Don't leave."

"You can't order me around, Ty. This is my life, not yours."

"That baby is *our* life, Marissa."

With that, he left her kitchen. With that, he took a

few gulps of fresh air. With that, he hurried down the steps of the shabby apartment building.

He had a son. Somehow he had to wrap his mind around the idea that he was a father—and then quickly decide what to do about it.

Chapter Two

Marissa's hand shook as she warmed Jordan's baby food and scooped it into a dish for him. Her own barbecued beef supper would be sitting in that skillet and serve her for the rest of the week. She had no appetite.

Would Ty come back tonight? Or had he just said that to keep her on alert, to keep her off balance? She was already way off balance. What was she going to do?

As she dipped the spoon into Jordan's food and made noises like an airplane to coax him to eat it, she wondered what Ty Conroy was going to do.

She'd seen the thunder in his eyes when she'd confirmed the fact that Jordan was his. That thunder was anger that she hadn't told him. She was pretty sure of that. With his lifestyle, she'd concluded he'd want nothing to do with a baby. She'd concluded he might never be back in Fawn Grove again. The circuit could take him anywhere, including to his best dreams. When he had enough money to fund his dreams, why would he want to come back to Fawn Grove? He could do or be anything he wanted. He could travel. He could have a different girl in each town and never get bored.

Ty had had a following of girls in high school. He'd been a wrestler and won a state championship his senior year. However, the book on him was that he didn't date much. When did he have time with wrestling practice and chores on the Cozy C? But when he did date, he dated a different girl every time. The thing was, the girls he dated only once still spoke highly of him. They still liked him. They said he was polite and charming and made them laugh. He was a good time.

Marissa knew for certain that he was a good time. She looked at Jordan and she remembered that night with Ty explicitly.

The knock on her door came less than fifteen minutes later. She answered it quickly, wanting to get the issue over with, wanting to get it resolved. If it was resolvable.

She'd wiped Jordan down. Somehow he always managed to dip his fingers into the bowl and then smear the gravy all over his face. Now he was sitting in his play saucer with its activity center, bouncing a bit, manipulating the buttons on a ring on one side of the play table. There were activities the whole way around the circle. His attention span was the strongest when he was playing there. *Her* attention span right now was zilch.

Her heart thudded hard as she let Ty in and wondered again what he was going to say. More important, what he was going to do.

"Would you like coffee?" she asked, maybe trying to postpone the inevitable. "I don't have any beer."

"Coffee's fine," he answered, removing his hat, laying it on the table. He ran his hand through his dark brown hair and she remembered running her fingers through it. It was thick but soft and silky. His body had been all hard muscle. Her eyes glided across his shoulders. He still was. There might even be more muscle definition in his arms.

She poured two mugs and set them on the table. "Black, right?" At least that's what she remembered from the reception.

"Right," he said with a crisp nod as he stared down at Jordan.

She added milk to her coffee, then a little sugar. When she sat, too, Jordan's saucer right beside her chair, she asked, "What did you decide on your walk?"

"No decisions, Marissa. I need the facts first."

She frowned, not sure what he meant. "What facts do you mean?"

"First of all, why didn't you tell me?"

She felt herself bristle and knew getting defensive wouldn't do either of them any good. How to explain this so he'd understand? How to explain this without turning herself inside out? She'd start with the simpler explanation.

"You're a rodeo cowboy, Ty. That's all you ever wanted to be. You told me that yourself over dinner at the wedding reception."

"Rodeo cowboys can't be fathers?" he asked in a low, controlled voice.

"How can they be when they're never around?"

Maybe that struck too close to home because a

shadow crossed his face and his jaw tightened. "You're generalizing."

"You've asked me a question and I'm trying to answer. Maybe *you* should answer a couple of questions. If I had told you I was pregnant, would you have seen me through my pregnancy? Would you have come back to Fawn Grove? Would you have been here during labor and delivery? Or if that had been the weekend of a big rodeo, would you have been *there* bull riding? I asked myself those questions and others. Would you quit the circuit? Would you willingly settle down? I came up with a resounding *no*."

"You didn't give me the chance to make up my own mind. You just sailed right by disclosure into doing it on your own. It takes two people to make a baby, Marissa, and I deserved to know."

She'd carried guilt from not telling Ty about the baby, sure she had. But as an unwed mother with nowhere to turn, she'd done the best she could.

"So you asked yourself about my rodeo life, and you decided that came first with me." He studied her. "But more was going on than that, wasn't it?"

"Sure, more was going on than that," she said, practically spilling her coffee mug in her agitation as she plopped it down. "This certainly wasn't a planned pregnancy. You had a life on the road and I had to find some way to make a life. What kind of parent could you have been if I'd trapped you into fatherhood? Wouldn't you have resented me? Wouldn't you have resented Jordan?"

Ty's expression was almost forbidding when he asked, "What makes you think I would have resented having a son?"

That question took precedent over all the others. Although she didn't want to delve into her past, she knew she had no choice if she wanted to make him understand.

She took a few sips of her coffee as a bracing elixir. She rarely talked about her childhood, but maybe she had to do it now to make Ty understand. She put her hand on Jordan's head, pushed her thumb through his hair, felt the warmth of his skin on her palm. This was her baby, her child, and she loved him dearly. Could Ty come to love him, too?

"My father married my mother because she was pregnant." The statement seemed to fall with a thud onto the table between them.

Ty's eyes widened a bit and then he nodded and said, "Go on."

She shouldn't have to go on. That should be enough. But he wanted it all laid out.

"They had an unhappy marriage. They argued all the time. Dad left for days at a time and didn't come back." From that she'd learned to distrust men. Because of her dad's example, she didn't believe they could commit to loving a family or stay.

She paused for a moment and then went on. "He didn't even care if he had a wife or a daughter, and I never felt loved. I wasn't about to put Jordan through that type of childhood."

Letting that go for the moment, Ty asked, "What happened?"

"Nothing monumental. But my parents split up. When my father left, I thought it was my fault. I knew they'd gotten married because of me. I'd heard the arguments, the conversations in the middle of the night.

Why else would he have left, after all? No child should have to bear that burden."

She felt tears come into her eyes, and she blinked fast and hard, not wanting Ty to see. She'd revealed more than enough.

Ty felt as though someone had clobbered him with a two-by-four. First of all, he couldn't look across the table at Marissa without being attracted to her. He couldn't look at her without thinking about their night together. It had been almost two years and it felt as if it had been yesterday. The chemistry that had arced between them back then hadn't flickered out. It was still sparking now in spite of this whole emotional upheaval, in spite of the fact she'd kept something so important from him, and he didn't know if he could ever trust her again.

Hearing her background had stirred up a locked box that he kept in a corner of his heart. It was locked because his childhood hadn't been much better. His background made him a lousy bet for a dad. His own father hadn't known how to handle responsibility. He hadn't known how to stay. Maybe he simply hadn't known how to love.

He wondered how Marissa had managed. She had been a waitress when they'd hooked up, he remembered. Had she done it on her own, or...

"Did your mom help?" he asked. "Is she helping you now?"

Marissa's voice was almost a whisper. "I lost my mom a few months before we hooked up. Maybe that's why that night happened. Maybe I just needed somebody to lean on."

She'd done more than lean on him, and they both knew it. But he kind of understood what she meant. Loss could make a person reckless. Loss of his career had almost made him reckless until he'd realized his uncle needed him, until he'd realized he could turn being reckless into a little bit of risk-taking and possibly hit a jackpot.

"So what did you do during your pregnancy? You were a waitress, living on tips and minimum wage." He motioned to the apartment. "How could you even afford this?"

"I didn't have anyone to count on during my pregnancy. But I attended a free clinic and Dr. Kaitlyn Foster, Kaitlyn Preston now, took care of me. I found out about The Mommy Club. It's a volunteer organization, and the women help parents in need. Sara Cramer, the physical therapist I was talking to when I saw you, is a member of The Mommy Club, too. They helped her."

"I don't get it. You didn't have to pay them?"

"There's no membership fee or anything like that. For example, Sara's house burned down. Jase Cramer offered her and her child his guest cottage until she got back on her feet. The Mommy Club helped provide clothes and furniture and anything else they needed. It's what the organization does. They help parents who can't make it on their own. I know this apartment isn't the greatest, but they found it for me. I can afford the rent. I've made it cheerful and upbeat for Jordan. I'm hoping to ask for a raise and look for a new place soon. But The Mommy Club made this life I have with him possible. They even have a day care set up. The fees are arranged on a sliding scale according to what you can afford to pay. I don't know what I'd do without them."

So Marissa didn't know what she'd do without The Mommy Club. He didn't like the idea of her depending on strangers. He didn't like the idea of someone else doing what was best for his child. She had done a nice job of prettying up the apartment, but it was what it was, and he wanted them living somewhere nicer. He wasn't exactly sure what he should do next.

Then suddenly he knew. "Can I hold Jordan?"

Marissa gave him an odd look, and he was about to spout the fact that he was the dad and had rights, when she explained, "He has a lot of energy and won't stay still very long. Let me get him out of his saucer and then we'll go from there."

Ty had to acquiesce to her wishes. After all, she knew her son. *Their* son.

Jordan wasn't happy when Marissa picked him up. The baby seemed fascinated with a blue elephant attached to the saucer. He squealed and kicked his legs until Marissa jiggled him, lifted him high up in the air and looked him straight in the eyes.

"I want you to meet somebody, big boy. Let's not show off how contrary you can be right now, okay?"

Jordan reacted to the sound of her voice, stopped kicking and stared at her face, then he broke into a wide smile and cooed.

Ty was entranced.

He'd never really watched a baby's antics before, and he was captivated, not only by Jordan but by the look on Marissa's face. Clearly she was devoted to this baby. With her dark brown curls tumbling around her face, her eyes sparkling with the joys of motherhood, she was absolutely beautiful. Beautiful in a way he hadn't recognized before. Did motherhood do that to a woman?

Now that Jordan was quieter, Marissa brought him into the crook of her arm again and approached Ty. She did not tell the little boy *This is your dad.*

Rather, she said, "I have somebody new I want you to meet." Marissa explained to Ty, "He's not usually shy about meeting new people. I think being at day care has done that. He just doesn't like to stay in one place for too long."

Her gaze met Ty's and held. He knew exactly what she was thinking. Like father like son? Up until a few months ago, that had certainly been true.

He might as well admit his nervousness. "I've never held a baby before."

Her lips quirked up and there was amusement in her eyes. "It's sort of the same as holding a baby calf. They're squiggly and want to get away."

That analogy brought an unexpected chuckle from him. "Okay." He'd held on to baby calves before.

Jordan was wearing a red shirt and denim overalls. One of the straps had slipped down his shoulder. Ty slipped his forefinger under it and straightened it.

Marissa was close enough that he caught the scent of her shampoo. Oh, how he remembered that scent. The night he'd made love to her, her hair had smelled like flowers, and that's the scent he caught now. It triggered a response in his body that was totally inappropriate for this situation. He willed himself to block off any attraction to Marissa. He knew how to concentrate. He'd had to focus hard when he got up on those bulls. Now he focused hard on Jordan.

"How'd you pick his name?" Ty asked to fill the air with more than the vibrations between the two of them.

"I liked it," she said simply.

He remembered again, no mom, no family, just The Mommy Club helping her, strangers helping her, and she was making a life for herself. Marissa Lopez was stronger than he ever imagined.

Taking the bull by the horns, so to speak, he slid his large hands under Jordan's little arms. Then he lifted the little boy from Marissa's hold. Jordan went perfectly still as Ty didn't know what to do with him once he had him. Then he remembered how Marissa had tucked him into the crook of her arm. So he tried that. His little boy's body was solid and warm.

His little boy.

Ty's chest constricted and his throat tightened. Just what in the blue blazes was happening to him?

Jordan looked up at him, seemingly mesmerized by Ty's face, and Ty was just as mesmerized with his son. Jordan reached out his hand and his fingers touched Ty's jaw. Ty now wished he'd shaved this morning. Would that little hand get scratched by beard stubble? His hand covered Jordan's to make sure it wouldn't.

Jordan smiled at him, the baby's eyes bright with the discovery of something new to do.

However, the quiet didn't last long. Jordan pulled his hand away and began squiggling, kicking his legs, rocking to and fro. Ty had to be quick to hold him securely.

"He's an armful," he mumbled.

"Especially when he wants to be somewhere else," Marissa confessed. "You can put him down."

"He can walk?"

"He has been since August. He was a fast crawler, but now he gets around even faster. Some days I think he can move like lightning."

Not wanting Jordan to be unhappy in his high perch,

or squiggling away and falling, Ty said, "Whoa, little guy. I'll put you down." But Ty realized that wasn't what he really wanted to do. He would have liked to keep holding the baby for a while, studying the face that seemed to be a mixture of his and Marissa's. Jordan definitely had her eyes, deep dark chocolate brown. But the mouth? That could have been Ty's.

Jordan toddled over to a laundry basket filled with toys. He lifted out a plastic bucket and threw it to the kitchen floor. Then he pulled out a stuffed dog and that landed next to the bucket.

"Will he empty the basket?" Ty asked, fascinated now by the baby's behavior.

"He'll empty it until he finds what he wants, or he'll empty it just because he wants to. I'm trying to teach him to put everything back in again, but you know how that goes."

"No, I don't."

Marissa blushed. "I didn't mean that the way it came out. I just meant—" She threw up her hands. "Oh, never mind."

"You meant that teaching him how to put toys away is hard. I get it, Marissa. But now I would like *you* to understand something. Jordan is my son, and I want to be his father. No, I'm not sure how that's going to play out yet, but I do know I want to spend time with him."

"What kind of time?" she asked, a bit shakily.

"I don't know. I want to think about it. Can I have numbers where I can reach you?"

After giving him a good long look, apparently deciding whether she wanted to acquiesce or not, she opened a drawer and took out a pad of paper and a pen.

Then she said, "I'll give you my cell number and my work number."

"Are you still waitressing at the diner?"

"Oh, no," she said, her pen stopping midnumber. "The Mommy Club helped me there, too. I needed a job with good insurance benefits. They hooked me up with Raintree Winery. Jase Cramer needed an assistant."

Jase Cramer was almost a celebrity in town. Ty read about him once when he'd accessed the local newspaper online. Cramer had been a photojournalist who'd won a Pulitzer. But he'd been shot while he was doing work in Kenya, and he'd come home to become general manager of Raintree Winery.

"Sara, his wife, is a physical therapist. You saw her talking to me," Marissa explained.

He thought how fortuitous it was to run into her at the facility. "Would you have ignored me if I hadn't called you over?" Ty couldn't help wondering just how long she would have kept his son from him.

"I don't know," Marissa said honestly. "I never expected to see you there. I never expected to see you back in Fawn Grove."

"So you don't know if you would have ended up on my doorstep with Jordan once the Cozy C is up and running? Certainly you would have heard I was back by then."

"I don't know, Ty. I can't tell you what I would have done and when." She hesitated a moment, then continued. "I didn't know you were back. Nobody knows that we're…connected in any way. No one but Sara and Kaitlyn, and they're as busy as I am and don't have time for gossip."

So she had two confidantes now. "They're close friends?" he asked.

"The best."

"And all three of you are involved in The Mommy Club?"

"We are."

Jordan banged a spatula he'd found in the wash basket against his bucket. As Ty tried to wrap his mind around Marissa's life, Marissa finished jotting down the numbers, and then she handed him the slip of paper so he could input them into his cell phone contacts. Their fingertips touched and Ty felt the electricity all over again—the quickening of his blood that had told him one night with this woman wasn't enough. But one night had led to a baby. Jordan had to be his main concern now. Not the chemistry he and Marissa might have.

When he stepped back, she seemed to breathe a sigh of relief. Because he was leaving?

"You might have kept me out of your life for two years, Marissa, but that's not how it's going to go now. I'm going to think about all this, then we can have a real discussion about what we're going to do next."

He crossed to Jordan and bent down to him. "Hey, little guy. I'm going to see you again soon."

Jordan studied him for a moment, then went back to slapping the spatula against the bucket. Maybe he was going to be a drummer.

Ty straightened and tucked Marissa's numbers into his shirt pocket. Then he crossed to the door and left.

His head was spinning as he stood outside Marissa's door feeling like the outsider he was. But that wouldn't be true for long. Nope. He was going to be Jordan's father. He just had to figure out how to do it.

* * *

As soon as Ty closed the door behind him, and Marissa heard his boots descending the steps, she scooped up Jordan and held him close. Tears came to her eyes because she didn't know what was going to happen next. What lengths would Ty go to in order to spend time with his son? Was he going to upset the steady balance she'd found?

Besides all that was the pull she still felt toward Ty Conroy. When they made eye contact, it was so hard for her to look away. It was so hard for her not to feel breathless, as if they'd started something they'd never finished.

Jordan had had enough of being held. He wiggled and squirmed until Marissa once more set him on the floor. Then he dug into that toy basket for something on the bottom.

Marissa needed advice and calm reason. Since Sara already knew Ty was back, she picked up her cell phone that was charging on the counter and speed-dialed Sara. When Sara answered, Marissa asked, "Are you busy?"

"We just finished dinner. Jase is playing a game with Amy on his tablet. What's up?"

Sara had been a widow and single mother when she'd met Jase. Now her little girl, Amy, adored him. He wasn't a stepfather. He was a real father.

"Ty came over. He put two and two together and came up with Jordan. His uncle knew I wasn't married and had a baby, so Ty filled in the blanks."

"Didn't you expect this to happen someday?" Sara asked reasonably.

"Denial's a wonderful thing, Sara. Knowing Ty's attitude and lifestyle, I just never expected I'd have to face it. So anytime I thought about Ty, I just pushed those thoughts away. I was living in a fool's paradise, I guess. Now it all crashed around me."

"What did he say?"

"His bull riding days are over. He and his uncle are turning the Cozy C into a vacation ranch. That's going to save the ranch for his uncle and give Ty employment."

"So he's staying in Fawn Grove."

"I guess. He's so used to being on the road, so used to traveling from place to place I just can't see him settled down. I can see him staying to get the ranch going, but then he could always find a general manager to run it if he found something else he wanted to do."

"Maybe he's grown wiser in the last two years," Sara suggested.

"You're the forever optimist, aren't you? But even if that's true, what does it mean if he stays? I don't know what he's going to want from me…from Jordan."

"Was he angry that you kept Jordan from him?"

"I think the anger was there, but it was underneath something else. I'm not sure what. I think he felt more disappointment than anything. But I explained why I didn't tell him and that seemed to help."

"So he's a reasonable man."

"I hope so. But to tell you the truth, Sara, I'm just concerned about what he might do next."

"How can I help?"

"No one can help. I'm just going to take this day by day and see what happens next."

"If you want Jase to step in—"

"No!" Marissa blurted out. "I know he's protective of me and Jordan, but I have to handle this on my own."

"Not on your own, Marissa. We're here for you—remember that."

Yes, they were here for her. But when Marissa examined her heart, she knew she and Ty had to come to terms with his fatherhood on their own.

Marissa gazed down at Jordan again and knew she didn't want to share him. She didn't want to lose any time with him. She didn't want to turn any part of his welfare—or her heart—over to a cowboy who might leave again.

Chapter Three

Ty drove for a while—not any place in particular, just on the back roads, circling the Cozy C. He was used to driving long distances from rodeo to rodeo. He was used to a lot of things.

But he wasn't used to holding a baby in his arms. *His* baby.

As daylight grew dimmer, he arrived back at the ranch, parked on the gravel lot near the house, then went in the kitchen door. In a hurry, he let the screen door slam behind him.

His uncle was at the stove, frying eggs. "I thought I'd go on and eat. You didn't tell me if you'd be back for supper."

He hadn't known when he'd be back. "I'm not hungry," Ty mumbled.

His uncle gave him one of those looks like the ones

he'd given him when he was a teenager and he'd been out too late. "You're always hungry. If you ain't got no appetite, then something's wrong. Spill it, boy."

Searching for the right words, Ty started with, "We have to make the Cozy C vacation ranch work." He paced the kitchen. "We can make sure the word gets out about it from Sacramento to San Diego. The best strategy is to make sure those cabins are what people want to live in for two days or a week. We can't just sit here and hope people find us. We have to spread the word somehow, just like a rodeo promoter does. In fact, maybe that's the route we should go. I have a lot of rodeo contacts who would recommend the Cozy C."

His uncle made sure his sunny-side up eggs were just right. "So what put a burr in your jeans now? We're not even finished with the cabins yet."

"We will be by Thanksgiving. I want to be open for business by January 1."

Eli glanced toward Ty's knee. "Are you sure you're going to be ready for that, especially if you intend to take out trail rides?"

"Another six weeks and I'll be as strong as I ever was." He pulled out a chair but didn't sit. Instead, he went to stand beside his uncle. "You've told me before that the Cozy C is my legacy. Well, I just found out tonight I have a son, and I want it to be *his* legacy, too."

Ty often saw his uncle silent, but never speechless. Now the older man looked shell-shocked as if he'd witnessed an explosion and didn't know what to do about it.

"Let's get your eggs and bacon on a dish and I'll tell you about it," Ty offered.

When they were seated at the table, after Ty had made himself a bacon-and-tomato sandwich, he began to bring his uncle up to speed. "Remember I told you I ran into Marissa Lopez?"

"Yeah. And I told you to stay away from her."

"Too late for that," Ty said matter-of-factly. "Two years ago after a wedding, she and I—" He slashed his hand through the air. "You know. Anyway, that baby you told me about? It turns out he's mine."

His uncle dipped his toast into the second egg, breaking the yolk. "I guess since you're telling me about it, since you're thinking about the Cozy C as an inheritance, you want to do something about being a dad."

"I held him for the first time tonight, Unc. I never felt anything quite like that. He's my flesh and blood. I have to make a future, not only for myself but for him, too."

His uncle swiped up more yolk with the crust of his toast. "How does the young'un's mom fit into this plan?"

Pushing his plate away, Ty shook his head. "I don't know how any of it fits together yet. She seems pretty self-reliant. She's working for Jase Cramer at Raintree Winery. Her momma died and she's got no family left, but The Mommy Club helped her."

Ty laid out what Marissa had told him about the organization.

"I've heard of it," Eli said. "They've had some goings-on in town. A Thanksgiving food drive is coming up. Lots of people talking about it. That's a good thing."

It was, and it seemed Marissa might be as involved as her friends because she felt she had to give back. He understood that, but he still didn't understand why she hadn't told him about Jordan.

"When are you going to see her again?" Eli asked.

"I'm not sure. I want to think about all of it."

"Apparently you've been thinking about the Cozy C, but not about what you're going to do with your son."

Maybe that was true. Maybe Ty felt if he planned for his own future, he'd be planning for his son's, and somehow Jordan would fit into his life.

"I want to try to work out visitation with her first. If we can't come to terms, then I guess I'll have to see a lawyer."

"You don't want to bring a lawyer into it if you don't have to," Eli agreed. "No better way to get two people on opposite sides of the fence."

Would Marissa work with him to decide what was best for Jordan?

"When am I going to meet my nephew?" Eli asked in a tone that said he wanted an answer now.

"I promise you'll meet him soon." Ty meant every word. He never broke a promise.

His uncle nodded because he knew that was true.

Ty's dad had broken too many promises, and his uncle realized Ty was determined to be a different kind of man than his father ever was.

On Saturday, Ty fully expected Marissa to be at home. But when he stopped at her apartment, he found no one was there. Sure, he should have called first, but he didn't want her avoiding him when she saw his name on caller ID. Did he really think she'd do that? Well, for two years she hadn't told him he had a son. He wasn't sure what she'd do.

Standing outside the door to her apartment, he dialed her cell phone number, fully expecting to get a message. But she answered on the second ring, and of course, she had seen who was calling.

"Ty? I'm at work. Can I call you back later?"

For some reason he didn't want to wait till later. He'd already missed too much time with his son. He wanted to make plans as soon as he could.

"How about if I come there and we can talk for a few minutes? I won't take up much of your time."

When she hesitated, he asked, "Where's Jordan?"

"He's with a friend, Kaitlyn Preston."

Kaitlyn Preston. He'd seen the name somewhere. Suddenly a doctor's shingle came to mind. Dr. Kaitlyn Preston had an office in the same building as his orthopedist. Then he remembered something else. Marissa had mentioned Kaitlyn in association with The Mommy Club.

Raintree Winery was about a mile out of town toward the hills. There was a rumor there was even a hot spring on the property. Hot springs. Marissa. A kiss. A touch. He shook the thoughts out of his head.

"I'll be there in less than ten minutes," he said.

And he was.

Driving down the lane into the winery, he passed scenery more manicured than the Cozy C's. There were rows and rows of trellises covered with grape vines as well as purple, white and yellow chrysanthemums blooming everywhere. He'd heard the vineyard was coming to be known for its gardens as much as for its grapes and wines. Visitors who stopped to taste Raintree wines also toured the beds of roses and native flowers and shrubs. The vineyard's property line on the western edge touched the Cozy C's north pasture.

Ty followed the visitors sign that led to the winery

offices. There was another driveway leading to the wine tasting center. He passed a guest cottage on the left and the main house on the right. That house was huge, more like a mansion compared to the ranch house on the Cozy C. Right past it he found the Raintree office complex, pulled into the designated parking area and switched off his ignition.

This was some place.

Ty walked up the path to the office, pulled open the heavy glass door and stepped inside. He didn't know what he expected, maybe to see Marissa sitting at a desk, welcoming any visitors who might come in.

But that wasn't the way it was. He spotted her through a glass partition. She was standing by a huge mahogany desk focused on a state-of-the-art computer monitor. He could tell by its size and sleek design. She wore tailored russet-brown slacks and a crisp pale peach blouse. She'd clipped her hair away from her face, but that didn't keep the curls from tumbling forward.

He felt the old attraction, and he attempted to ignore it.

She wasn't alone in her office. A man about as tall as Ty stood there with her, handing her some kind of printout. He was well built with black hair. He wore a white oxford dress shirt and navy suit trousers. Ty recognized him. Jase Cramer's photo had appeared online and in newspapers with his articles about children in African refugee camps.

Ty hadn't been oblivious to the world outside the rodeo circuit. After all, a Pulitzer Prize winner made headlines.

He strode toward the office. Marissa glanced up, and the glass walls seemed to drop away. It was just the two of them, staring at each other, wondering what the future was going to bring.

She had stopped midsentence apparently and Jase looked from her to Ty and then back again.

"This is the man you were expecting?" he heard Jase ask her through the open door.

She motioned him in. "Jase Cramer, meet Ty Conroy. Ty, this is my boss."

As Ty shook Jase Cramer's hand, he was sizing him up, and Jase was doing the same thing to Ty.

Jase turned to Marissa. "Would you like to go someplace more private than this?"

Marissa's cheeks pinkened. "No, this is fine. Thanks."

"We're almost there, Marissa. You've done a terrific job planning the Christmas-week celebration. You've managed to get great vendors on board, and the publicity you generated is acquiring lots of interest. We're good. Don't let the odds and ends tie you up in knots, okay?"

She nodded.

After a last smile for Marissa and a nod to Ty, Cramer left the office. Just outside the door, he said, "I'll be in the wine tasting room if you need me for anything."

Again Marissa nodded and then she laid the papers on her desk.

"The Christmas celebration," Ty mused aloud. "That's a big event at Raintree. A big event in the area. Visitors go hopping from one winery to the next. You have to plan it?"

"I planned it," she said proudly, "consulting with Jase and Sara, of course, and the other wineries in the area. That's one of the things I do here, Ty. I plan the events."

He must have made a sound of surprise or looked

surprised because Marissa's shoulders went back and
she stood a little straighter. "Did you think I'd stay a
waitress in a diner all my life?"

He realized he'd underestimated Marissa. Apparently becoming pregnant and having a baby had made
a huge difference in her life.

"Girls in Fawn Grove who start out as waitresses
usually end up as waitresses. I really didn't know what
your life goals were. We didn't talk about that."

She seemed to relax a bit. "No, we didn't. The ironic
thing is I took this job for the insurance benefits. And
when I started, I was basically Jase's secretary." She
motioned to the office beyond hers. "That's where he
works. But as the months went on, I handled more and
more responsibility, and he saw that I really seemed
suited for everything that goes on here, from setting
up the wine tasting schedule to incorporating holiday
themes in the gardens, to planning everything from an
ice-cream festival to a music fair. I quickly moved up. I
like the work I do here, and even more than that, I like
the people I work with."

Ty nodded. "That's important. One of my friends
from the rodeo circuit who wants to retire is going to
hire on with us at the Cozy C. Clint and I have known
each other since my first rodeo. He's good with horses
and anything else that needs to be done."

"I guess you have a lot on your plate right now, too,"
she said, "getting ready for the opening."

"It's coming together. Uncle Eli wasn't 100 percent
on board at the beginning, but I think that's changing.
I sure hope it is."

"So your uncle doesn't want to turn the Cozy C into
a dude ranch?" she asked with an amused smile.

"We're calling it a vacation ranch," Ty corrected her with a wink.

"I see." She was still looking a bit amused and her eyes were twinkling.

She was so darn pretty. But he wasn't here to talk about the ranch, and he wasn't here to flirt. "I won't hold you up. I know you're busy."

Now that twinkle was gone from her eyes. In fact, he thought he could see fear there. What was she afraid of?

"Uncle Eli wants to meet Jordan, and I want to spend some time with him. How about coming to the ranch for dinner tonight?"

As Marissa drove her six-year-old small sedan down the winding road that led to the Cozy C, she noticed the fresh-laid stones crunching under her tires. She also spotted new fence posts along the fence line that ran by the side of the road.

Jordan rattled the plastic play keys that were attached to his car seat.

"We're almost there, buddy."

Those butterflies in her stomach seemed to be doing the salsa the closer she got to the ranch. She'd known she had to attend this dinner tonight. It was only fair. But what was going to happen next? That's what those butterflies were all about.

Ty had said he wanted to spend time with his son. Did he mean just tonight? Or was he talking more long-term than that? Just the thought of seeing him again made her palms sweat. She took a couple of deep breaths warning herself to calm down. She wouldn't want to hyperventilate in front of his uncle—or in front of Ty for that matter.

The lodgepole pines, fir trees and aspens gave the ranch a look similar to Raintree Winery. She'd never had wide-open spaces around when she was a kid. She'd been unaware of what gardens could do for a property or how wildflowers just made one want to sigh and relax. She was fortunate to work at Raintree, and she realized how fortunate Ty was that he could renovate the Cozy C with his uncle. He had family that mattered and a place that mattered. Did he realize how important that was?

Spotting a truckload of lumber covered loosely by a tarp, she realized some construction was still going on here. Just when would the Cozy C open for guests?

She let thoughts like that occupy her as she approached the ranch house. It was three stories, but judging by the small windows in the two dormers, that third story could be an attic, she supposed. A wide porch surrounded the first floor on three sides. The banisters were freshly painted white. The light gray siding and black shutters also looked new. Even the steps leading up to the porch were a shiny gray. The landscaping around the steps looked as if it was in the process of a makeover, though young shrubs were positioned along the home's foundation, and the beds appeared newly mulched. She just caught a glimpse of the pasture beyond and a few horses running there.

"Horses, buddy. What do you think of that?" Marissa asked her son.

His answer was "Mmm, momma momma momma."

She smiled as she parked.

It was time to pretend she was confident, self-assured and totally self-reliant. She climbed out of the car, unhooked Jordan from his car seat and hiked him into her arms. Then she managed to snag the diaper bag, which went with her everywhere. After she ran up the porch steps, she rang the doorbell. She could smell the newly painted wood.

When the door opened, she expected to see Ty. But instead an older man with a weathered face appeared. Eli Conroy, she assumed. His hair receded from his forehead and gray laced the brown there as it did on his beard. He wore overalls and a plaid shirt and didn't look any too happy to see her.

"I guess you're Marissa," he said. "You're early."

Automatically she glanced at her watch. She couldn't be more than ten minutes early.

"I never know how long it will take to get Jordan and his necessities together. So I always try to start out sooner than I need to."

Eli Conroy looked her up and down, then his expression seemed to gentle as his eyes fell on Jordan.

"Come on in." He beckoned her through the living room into the kitchen. "Ty should be here any minute. He got tied up with a problem at one of the guest cabins and is getting a shower."

All of a sudden Marissa heard movement beyond the archway on the left side of the kitchen. Then she heard Ty's voice. "That new shower works great, Unc. Don't tell me you don't like to just be able to step in there and—"

"She's here early," Eli said, motioning to Marissa.

Marissa felt totally dumbfounded. Not because Ty had appeared in the kitchen, but because he'd appeared in the kitchen shirtless with his hair still wet and with a few drops of water clinging to his curling chest hair. She knew her eyes were glued to him, but she couldn't seem to look away. When she did manage to avert her gaze, her eyes collided with his and caught. Two years rolled back. She recalled running her fingers through that chest hair, inhaling deep breaths of his masculine scent, melding with him until she didn't know where she began or he ended.

Eli cleared his throat, took a step forward and held his arms out to Jordan.

"Will you come to me?" he asked gruffly.

Memories of Ty and their night together scattered as all of her concern focused on Jordan. Eli was a stranger to him. Would her son cry?

But he didn't cry. He leaned forward and Eli took him. Jordan reached for Eli's beard and took it in his fist, giggling.

Eli chuckled, too.

Ty's eyebrows quirked up and he grinned. "Not just anybody takes to Uncle Eli. Jordan must be a good judge of character."

Eli harrumphed. "I can take Jordan on a little tour of the porch. Maybe you should show Marissa here that old high chair and see if it's suitable for this young'un."

"I can do that," Ty agreed. He touched her elbow. "It's upstairs. I pulled it down from the attic and cleaned it up last night."

Marissa was about to say that she could unfasten Jordan's car seat and bring that in for him to sit in, but there was something in Ty's look that said he wanted her to see this high chair.

She followed him through the living room to the staircase there. Even barefoot Ty was still a good six inches taller than she was. She glanced over her shoulder at her son and saw he was babbling to Eli. That was a good sign, she supposed.

As she climbed the steps behind Ty, her gaze kept wandering to his broad back, his strong spine, his muscled arms. It seemed awkward, this silence between her and Ty. So she asked, "Did you say your uncle has a new shower?"

At the top of the stairs, Ty turned toward her to wait until she reached the landing.

"When we decided to make renovations, I wanted Uncle Eli to have a bedroom and shower downstairs so when his arthritis was bothering him, he didn't have to climb the steps. That little suite seems to be the one thing he likes about this whole Cozy C makeover. It's convenient for him and I don't have to worry about him falling on the stairs."

"That sounds like a great idea. Jase and his father did something similar. That way he and Sara have an apartment on the second floor."

"You're close to them?" Ty asked.

"They're good friends."

He gave her a long studying look and led her down the hardwood floors of the hallway to the last bedroom on the left.

"This is sort of a storage room, so don't expect a lot of order. One of the neighbors, Hannah Johnson, comes in, cleans and leaves casseroles in the freezer for Eli. He grumbles about it because she only takes a pittance. But she's a widow and says she needs something to do since her husband died."

"That's kind of her," Marissa said, but she wondered if there was more behind it. Maybe this Hannah was sweet on Eli?

When Ty opened the door to the room, a stale smell wafted out. Apparently they didn't open the windows much in here. There wasn't a bed. Boxes were stacked here and there, and in the corner by the closet, she spotted the high chair.

"It's solid maple," Ty explained. "Eli made it for me when I was a baby. Apparently my mother would bring me to visit him a few weeks in the summer."

"Eli used to do woodworking?"

"A long time back. Arthritis in his hands has kept him from it for the past decade."

Crossing to the high chair, she ran her hands over the smooth, glossy wood. It had a beautiful grain. Even the tray was wood. It smelled of lemon polish.

"It's beautiful, Ty. It seems to be a perfect size for Jordan."

They were standing very close, Ty's bare arm brushing hers. He said, "I don't have much ready for my son yet, but I will."

"Babies have a lot of paraphernalia, but they really don't need much," she murmured.

"You'll have to tell me what kind of food to buy, what kind of diapers, that kind of thing," Ty said in a low voice, not taking his eyes from her face.

She couldn't seem to look away from him, either. "Why do you think you'll need all that?" she asked, her heart beating very fast. Just what did he have in mind?

"When I bring Jordan here to stay—"

She cut him off. "I can't be away from him for long periods of time. As it is, he's in day care all day. If you just visit him at my apartment, won't that be enough?" After all, this was Ty Conroy. When he wasn't rodeoing, he met his friends for a beer in a sports bar like the Black Boot.

"Look, Marissa, my life has changed drastically.

Now Jordan's going to be a part of it. We'll work this out. But he's going to spend time here with me and Uncle Eli. The Cozy C could be his someday."

She knew she made a little sound of surprise.

"We have to think ahead now," he said. "Maybe you've just been living day to day, but that's going to change."

Confusion stole through Marissa's heart. She liked to think of herself as flexible. But when it came to Jordan, she didn't know how flexible she could be.

Ty pushed a few curls away from her cheek. "I'm going to learn how to become a father, Marissa, so I'd like you to try and get used to that idea."

His callused fingers on her cheek made her insides quiver and her knees even felt a little weak. Or maybe that was because everything was happening so fast. Maybe because seeing Ty in a father's role wasn't something she ever expected to do.

Ty stepped back and she felt relieved. When he was that close she had trouble fighting her attraction to him. When he was that close anything could happen.

He hefted up the high chair and nodded to the doorway. She crossed to it, eager to go downstairs and get dinner over with, eager to go back to her apartment with Jordan.

Ty put a shirt on before he came to the table, but all through dinner she couldn't keep her gaze from flitting to him. Just as she felt his eyes on her. She kept herself busy feeding Jordan. She'd brought along food for him, but also fed him bits of broccoli and the boiled potatoes with butter Eli had made.

After he'd eaten, she started on the barbecued ribs. In

between bites, she asked, "What did you use on these? They're delicious."

"I make my own rub," Eli said. "And I do them slow in the oven, basting them often. Ty's talking about getting one of those smokers, thinks guests might like it. But I like the way I do it."

"I make my own barbecue sauce," Marissa said. "Is your rub a secret?"

Eli chuckled. "Not so secret. I can jot it down for you."

When Ty put dessert on the table, Marissa remarked to Eli, "You're serving a feast."

"I can't take credit for the cherry crumble," Eli told her. "A neighbor made that for us."

Jordan had smeared his supper from one end of his mouth to the other and got some on his cheek and his nose. She reached out to clean him, but Ty stopped her. "Do you think he'll let me wipe him?"

"You can try. He doesn't even let me wipe his face sometimes."

Ty went to the counter and wet a paper towel. Moments later he was back, making a game of it with Jordan, wiping one cheek and tickling his tummy. Then he wiped the other, making a noise like an airplane while he did it.

Eli leaned close to Marissa. "Sometimes dads have the magic touch."

She felt as if Ty and Eli were tag-teaming her, trying to convince her of something. She wasn't sure what that was. That Ty would be a good father? Only time would tell that. Only time and Ty's commitment to his son.

As she looked at him, she still saw the rakish cowboy who flitted from town to town as if he'd never be-longed anywhere.

Could Ty Conroy make a commitment?

That was the question she had to answer before she could let him fully into her son's life.

Chapter Four

After supper, Ty and his uncle stepped into the living room for a few minutes while Marissa washed Jordan's hands. Their voices were low and their discussion made her nervous. Were they talking about her and Jordan?

Neither seemed ruffled when they returned to the kitchen. Eli was even smiling.

Ty glanced at her, then ruffled his son's hair. "Let me take you on a tour of the ranch."

Supper had gone well, Marissa decided. She didn't know if she wanted to push her time here further. Yet watching Ty act like a father to his son was fulfilling to witness—his gentleness, his concern, his caring.

She motioned to the dirty dishes. "We should clean up."

Without hesitation, Eli stepped into the argument. "No need. Since Ty got me that fancy new dishwasher, everything practically cleans itself. Go on. When you get back, you can let me know if anybody would come here for a vacation."

Ty was already gathering Jordan from the high chair.

"I have his collapsible stroller in the car," Marissa said. She took it everywhere. Forethought was a mom's friend.

"We'll be fine," Ty assured her, jiggling Jordan a little and making him giggle.

As they walked out onto the porch, he said, "He's a happy baby, isn't he?"

"Most of the time. Especially when he gets his way."

Ty chuckled and descended the steps. As they crossed to the barn, Marissa asked, "How's your knee?"

He shot her a glance. "I won't trip and fall with Jordan," he remarked with a bit of an edge.

"That wasn't my concern," she said softly.

He looked away toward the hills in the distance as if he was imagining riding there. "Sometimes I work it too hard," he admitted. "And that puts me back to using a cane. But there's so much I want to get finished by the end of the year."

Seeing that talking about his knee made him uncomfortable, she motioned toward the barn. "It looks good. It's a wonder what a new coat of paint will do."

"I wanted to have it sided or something more permanent, but Unc wouldn't hear of that."

"Did you say you won the biggest purse of your life the night of the accident?"

"Accident is a nice way of putting it," he said wryly. "But yes, I did, and most of the other winnings I'd socked away in the bank. After all, I didn't have many expenses on the road, or much I wanted to buy. When I was recuperating, I put most of it into building up the Cozy C and paying back taxes. Unc didn't tell me he was in trouble before that, or I would have helped sooner. He can be stubborn."

She cleared her throat. "And his nephew didn't inherit that fine quality."

Now Ty laughed and reached to open the barn door.

When she passed by him up the step into the barn, Jordan reached out and grabbed her cotton blouse. His little fist clamped on her sleeve. Her hand reached for Jordan's at the same time Ty's did. As their skin touched, Marissa felt a tremble the whole way through her body. Something about Ty Conroy shook her up, attracted her, made her feel so much like a woman.

She dropped her hand as Ty gently pried Jordan's fingers away from her sleeve.

"He likes me close by," she commented, trying to hide her reaction to Ty.

"He's not the only one." Ty's voice was low, almost a thought rather than a statement. He went on to say, "You always smell so good."

She tried not to take in his scent along with the smells of new wood, hay and horses. She didn't know what to say so she said nothing and moved forward.

The barn was part new, part old. Some of the stall doors were new lumber. Others were worn, dark and well grained. She noticed an enclosure that appeared new. The door stood open and she glimpsed tack inside.

"It looks as if you've done a lot of repairs and made some changes."

"We never had a tack room before, but we need one now if we're going to take parties out on trail rides. I have to go into town or to an auction and pick up new saddles."

"So many details."

"You bet. The guest cabins are almost finished. I mostly have just staining to do there."

She motioned around the barn. "Did you do some of this work yourself?"

"I did. I often worked construction jobs in between rodeo gigs when there was a time lag."

Marissa thought about how long Ty had been bull riding, the places he'd seen and the people he'd met. She tried not to think about the women he'd met.

"You've been all over the country, and I've never been out of California," she mused aloud.

"Do you want to get out of California?" he asked with a tilt of his head.

She had once dreamed of visiting faraway places. But that was before she'd become a mom. "I like Fawn Grove. It's always been my home. But I would like to see some sights other than photos on my smartphone."

Jordan was leaning toward the horses, and Ty walked over to one of the stalls. "I imagine you'd like Jordan to see them, too."

"Of course. I want him to see the world. But not too soon," she added in a teasing tone.

When Ty let Jordan get close to the horse, Marissa was concerned. Glancing at her, he must have seen that.

"Goldie is gentle," he assured her. "She doesn't move suddenly and not much rattles her. It will be safe for him to touch her."

"What kind of horse is she?"

"A Tennessee walker. A gaited horse. That makes riding easier for me. She and I have gotten along like best friends since I brought her here."

Marissa stepped up beside Ty, not knowing what to

expect from a horse, either. "Are you sure she won't bite or anything?"

She could tell Ty was trying to keep from laughing. "She won't bite," he assured her. "I guess you haven't been around horses much, either."

"Never been around them." They really were magnificent creatures, but so magnificent they scared her.

"We don't want Jordan to be afraid of them, right?"

"Right," she agreed, but without much enthusiasm. A little fear could be a healthy thing.

Ty took Jordan's little hand and guided it toward Goldie's nose. When the boy's fingers smoothed over the softness, he giggled and gave an excited sound of glee.

"Try it again," Ty said. "Anything that causes that reaction should be tried more than once."

Marissa's quick glance at him made her breath catch. There was something in Ty's eyes that said he remembered their night together as vividly as she did. Was there some message in what he'd said to Jordan?

"Now your turn," Ty told her. "Just run your hand down her nose and pat her neck. She likes that."

He made it all sound so sensual, like so much more than learning to know a horse.

When she reached out her hand, Ty advised her, "Slowly. Never move too fast around them. They're just like people, really. They don't like to be startled."

As she moved her hand over Goldie's nose, she could see why Jordan had giggled. It was a kind of softness she hadn't felt before.

Remembering what Ty had said, she slipped her hand around to the horse's neck. Her coat was coarse but pleasant to the touch. Her mane was silkier than the rest of her coat as it fell over Marissa's hand.

Although the horse had fascinated Jordan when they'd begun, now he was tired of being held and tired of touching Goldie's nose. He began shifting away from Ty.

"Is it okay if I put him down over near those hay bales? There's nothing he can get into and nothing that will hurt him there."

"Unless he starts eating the hay," Marissa said wryly.

Ty lowered Jordan to the floor.

The toddler looked around as if he'd just been placed in a whole new world. Then he staggered toward a hay bale, eager to touch it.

As they stood at the stall together, Ty's elbow brushed Marissa's. That quickening in her breath was back. He was so tall, so elementally male.

As they watched Jordan hold on to one bale and then toddle to another, Ty said, "That apartment building you're living in is getting run-down. What happens when you need a repair?"

Marissa wrinkled her nose. "It takes a couple of weeks till the landlord gets around to it. I had a leaky sink and Kaitlyn's husband, Adam, fixed it for me. I either do it myself or find a way around it."

"A child needs some space to move around, needs to see something other than the inside of an apartment, don't you think?"

Uh-oh. She should have left before the tour. "What are you getting at, Ty?"

He set his hat back farther on his head. "The Cozy C has always been a refuge to me. When I was a kid and things weren't going right, I could come out here to the horses. I could take walks through the fields. I could go on a hike through the hills."

The anxiety Marissa had felt driving out here became palpable, tightening a fist around her heart, making it hard to swallow. But she managed to say, "If you think I'm going to let Jordan come here and live with you, you're wrong. He's my son, Ty. He needs me."

"Calm down," Ty assured her gently. "Of course he does. I'm not suggesting Jordan come live here. I'm suggesting the *two* of you come live here. Think about it. It certainly would help you with expenses. You could save money for Jordan's future."

She was already shaking her head.

He cupped her shoulders so she'd look at him. "You kept Jordan's birth from me. I've lost fourteen months with him. Don't you see I want to know Jordan in a real way, not just sometimes, now and then, here and there?"

Looking deep into Ty's blue eyes, she tried to see the truth. Although Ty's rodeo days were over, would he really stay? Yes, he was committed to revamping the Cozy C. He seemed committed to his uncle. But could she trust him? Could she trust him to be the dad he wanted to be? Could she trust him not to just run off again, chasing some other dream?

"I was going to ask Jase for a raise and find a new place," she admitted.

"Ask him for a raise. I'm sure you deserve it. But as far as finding a new place... Think about the Cozy C. We have plenty of room here."

"Once you start taking on guests, everything will change."

"Sure, there might be people around," he said. "But the nature of the ranch won't change. Wouldn't it be good for Jordan to meet people from all walks of life? Wouldn't it be good for him to have me and Uncle Eli around him? We're family, Marissa, whether you like the idea or not."

Did she like the idea? "Your uncle might not want us around."

"You seem to get along with him. That's a feat in itself. He has his own set of rooms. He can be private when he wants to be private. I talked to him about it before we came out here. He's open to it, Marissa. I want you to be open to it, too."

Open to what exactly? Living under the same roof as Ty? Fighting her attraction to him? Open to being a family?

"I don't know."

"Think about it, Marissa. Think about the holidays here. A tall tree in the living room, wreaths on the doors, bells on the barn. Wouldn't Jordan love that?"

Just then, Jordan squealed and they both looked toward him. A kitten had dashed out from between the hay bales. He toddled after it laughing, excited, his eyes twinkling with a child's penchant for exploring.

Ty went over to him, sat down on the stack of hay bales and scooped up the kitten. He held it as Jordan stared at it wide-eyed.

He let Jordan touch the kitten, watching carefully, the same way that he'd watched over him as he'd touched the horse's nose.

Could Ty be a good dad? Would living here be good for Jordan?

Marissa knew her impulses had gotten her in trouble with Ty once before. The repercussions would be lifelong. On the other hand, she had to be open to what was best for Jordan.

She had a whole lot to think about.

Ty was holding Jordan again as he and Marissa walked back to the house. He realized how much more he wanted to hold him. How he wanted Marissa and Jordan here at the Cozy C where he could be a hands-on dad. After watching the expressions on his son's face, seeing him toddle around, Ty felt emotions in his heart he'd never experienced before. Did every dad have that deep, gut-wrenching desire to be part of his son's life?

He wanted to give Marissa more reasons she should stay at the Cozy C. But he knew he couldn't push, because if he did, he'd push her away. She'd become protective of her life and Jordan's, and they'd have to draw up some kind of visitation agreement. He didn't want that.

Just like rehab and working strength back into his muscles, everything took patience and time. He just wasn't feeling very patient right now.

Close to the house now, Ty spotted a sleek black sedan parked next to Marissa's car. As they entered the kitchen, he noticed the stranger right away. Dressed in a pale blue dress shirt, navy tie, expensive-looking dress slacks and shiny black loafers rather than boots, the blond man was almost as tall as Ty and maybe a few years older. Ty didn't like the fact that the man's green-eyed gaze went to Marissa and settled there.

Jordan had had enough of being carried, and he squawked a bit until Marissa went to the diaper bag on the counter and pulled out a set of blocks. She put them on the floor and he set Jordan down beside them. The baby was immediately entranced with them.

When he faced his uncle, Eli explained, "This is Scott Donaldson. He thinks I should sell the Cozy C to him."

Donaldson extended his hand to Ty. "Scott Donaldson, and you're—"

"Ty Conroy, Eli's nephew."

He gave that a bit of thought, and then his attention turned to Marissa. "And you are?" His voice held a note that Ty didn't like at all. It was that male appreciation note, that I-could-be-interested-in-you note.

"Marissa Lopez," she said, and that was all.

But Donaldson cocked his head and stepped incrementally closer. "Are you the Marissa Lopez who plans events for Jase Cramer?"

"You know Jase?"

"We're both members of the Chamber of Commerce. We worked on a committee together. I attended the festival at his winery in the summer, as well as several wine tastings. You set up the festival from what I understand."

"I did," she said proudly.

Donaldson's smile grew wider. "I also heard about the bachelor auction you planned for The Mommy Club. That was a big hit."

"We raised a nice amount of money," she agreed.

"Intelligent, capable and modest, too."

Marissa blushed a little, and Ty felt like pushing the man out the door.

"I have other business to discuss with Eli, but first I

have a question for you. You plan events for the winery. Do you ever plan events for private clients?"

"I never have," she admitted. "I didn't start out planning events for Jase. My job just evolved into that."

"And apparently you're very good at it," Donaldson complimented her again. He took a card from his pocket and handed it to her.

Marissa took it and studied it. "You're a property developer. I don't quite understand what you'd want me to plan," she said.

"I'd like to host a cocktail party at my house before Christmas for some important contacts. Do you think you'd be interested in doing something like that?"

In the next few quiet seconds, Ty realized exactly what Marissa was thinking. A fee like that could be nice to sock away for the future, not to mention to help pay some bills. And in the end a cocktail party like that could lead to other private events.

"I don't know how Jase would feel about this," she said honestly. "I'll have to talk to him about it."

"Fair enough," Donaldson said with a smile and a nod. "That's the best way to do business—up front."

Now Donaldson targeted Ty. "I understand you've been transforming this place into a dude ranch. The back taxes have been paid, and the property is now in decent condition. I'm interested in buying it."

"And undoing everything we've just done?" Ty asked, with a bit of edge to his voice.

"That would depend on the buyer," Donaldson confessed. "But does that really matter if you profited enough from the property?"

Obviously this man didn't have an understanding

of roots or memories, of a childhood spent here when there was nowhere else to go. He didn't understand what Goldie and the other horses meant. He could never understand that having the dust of a property like this on your boots was important.

Although Ty had funneled money into the place, the property was his uncle's to sell. He looked toward Eli now, hoping his uncle felt the same about it as he did.

"He named a nice sum, Ty," Eli said. "If I ever needed elder care…"

"You don't have to worry about that," Ty said gruffly. "I told you that before."

Eli studied Ty carefully as if he was judging the determination behind his commitment. Then he said to Donaldson, "I'll discuss this more with my nephew. We certainly won't make an impulsive decision. For now, we'd like to get the place up and running as the Cozy C Vacation Ranch."

"I'm a patient man," Donaldson said. "If you don't start drawing clients in for spring and summer, you might want to rethink your plans." He nodded to Ty. "It was good to meet you, Mr. Conroy. I heard you used to be the best bull rider in the state."

Before Ty could respond, Donaldson turned to Marissa. "I'll give you a call after Thanksgiving. If we want to do a Christmas cocktail party, I imagine we'll have to get moving on it."

When Ty looked at Donaldson, he wondered what Marissa saw. Did she see a snake-oil salesman? Or a successful man in expensive clothes who had a life that wasn't as hard as hers, that wasn't as hard as Ty's. If she wanted a better future for her and Jordan, would she seriously consider a man like Scott Donaldson if Donaldson was interested in *her*?

Ty didn't know where those thoughts had come from. He didn't even know if Marissa had dated anyone since Jordan had been born. She was beautiful. It seemed obvious that she would have.

Marissa smiled at Donaldson and it appeared to be a genuine smile. She said, "I promise I'll talk to Jase."

As Donaldson left, with the door banging behind him, Ty felt disconcerted and annoyed.

Eli said, "I'm going to watch some TV. We can talk about Donaldson's offer later. There's certainly no hurry." To Marissa he said, "You've got a fine boy there. Don't be a stranger." Then he turned and went into the living room.

Jordan was still pushing the blocks around, running one of them on the floor as if it were a car.

"He was flirting with you," Ty said, in a low voice. "Working for him could only lead to trouble."

As soon as he said the words, he knew that had been the wrong way to go about it.

Marissa's brown eyes flashed. "That's my decision to make."

That was true, but she had to be reasonable. "How much time are you going to have for Jordan if you start taking on private clients?"

"Are you opposed to private clients or are you opposed to Scott Donaldson?"

"Maybe I'm opposed to both. Whether you come here to live or not, I have a say in anything that involves Jordan. Are we clear on that?"

But this time she pushed back. "Don't think you can just drop into Jordan's life and suddenly change mine."

"You kept him from me for fourteen months."

At that accusation, she blew out a breath. Then she said, "You're right. I did. Maybe I was wrong. Maybe you have what it takes to be a dad. I watched you with Jordan tonight. You seem to be good with him."

They both turned to look at their son, their shoulders brushing, their tempers suddenly short-circuited. When they looked at each other again, the sizzle was back, the pull was back, the desire to fold her into his arms was back. He leaned toward her and he could have sworn she leaned toward him.

But then she stepped away. "What if I come to live here, and then your uncle decides to sell the Cozy C?"

"That's not going to happen."

She studied him, glanced into the living room at Eli, and then at Jordan. "I'd better go. I'll think about it."

She'd think about it and so would he. Having her in a room down the hall could be a temptation he couldn't resist. But he might have to if he wanted to be a dad.

Kaitlyn's invitation to dinner on Sunday evening at her and Adam's new house was the answer to one of Marissa's prayers. As an environmental geologist, Adam was at a meeting at the Sacramento college where he taught. Marissa would take Jordan, of course, but Sara would be there, too, for a girls' night, as Jase was taking care of their daughter, Amy. The three of them could have an honest, confidential talk.

Kaitlyn and Adam's house was the type of home they'd both always wanted, so they could put down roots and start their family. The fireplace added a homey touch.

When Marissa arrived, she asked Kaitlyn, "How are you feeling?"

Still early in her pregnancy, Kaitlyn looked well and even more important, she looked happy. "I'm good. Adam makes sure I get at least eight hours of sleep, and we both monitor my diet."

Sara had arrived too, and all three women laughed.

Jordan toddled up to Marissa to snatch a stuffed blue elephant from her hand and carried it over to Kaitlyn's sofa where he danced it across the cushions.

Sara pitched in. "Jase told me Adam is so excited about the baby. Every time he goes out shopping he brings home a new stuffed toy."

"We already have a nursery full of them," Kaitlyn admitted. "I can empty out the crib if you'd like to put Jordan down to sleep."

"I don't want to use your new crib," Marissa protested.

"Nonsense," Kaitlyn said. "Cribs are bought to be used. He can try it out, then we'll know if it's comfortable."

"Do you have any more gigs on TV shows?" Marissa asked, teasing their friend.

The Mommy Club had asked Kaitlyn to represent the organization on a statewide public relations campaign. The objective was to start Mommy Clubs in more towns, so parents and children could be helped by a free summer lunch program, charitable donations, aid after a tragedy, babysitting services and affordable care for moms and kids. There was so much a Mommy Club could do in any town.

"Actually Adam and I are going down to LA next weekend, where I'm taping an interview. I think he's more excited about it than I am. Working part-time at the practice is working out nicely. Once the baby's born, I'll still be able to be a pediatrician and a mom, too."

"And Adam is happy teaching?" Sara asked.

Adam had changed his life for love. Once an environmental geologist traveling the world, he'd taken a professorship at a college to start his family and plant roots.

"He's good at teaching," Kaitlyn said. "He says the college kids keep him on his toes. He always likes a good challenge."

"That's why he married you," Sara quipped, and they all laughed again. Sara focused her attention on Marissa. "And how are you doing?"

That was the opening she needed, so she might as well take advantage of it.

Kaitlyn sent Marissa a questioning glance. "Does Sara know something I don't?"

"Ty Conroy's back in town. He's been back for a couple of months, and I didn't even know it. I ran into him at the physical therapy practice when I stopped in to see Sara. Talk about shock."

Kaitlyn looked totally concerned now. "What happened?"

"Nothing right then," Marissa assured her. "But his uncle mentioned I had a baby, and Ty put two and two together and came to see me. So I told him the truth."

Kaitlyn whistled low. "So what's happening?"

Marissa explained how Ty's bull riding days had ended, and how the Cozy C was being turned into a vacation ranch. "He wants me to move in with him and his uncle. He wants time with Jordan."

Sara and Kaitlyn exchanged a look. "How do you feel about it?" Sara asked.

"I'm scared. If I don't move in, he could file for some kind of custody agreement. I don't have money to pay a lawyer, and don't tell me The Mommy Club would help. I know that, but I'd rather avoid a lawyer getting involved."

"So you're thinking about moving in?" Kaitlyn asked.

"The thing is, the Cozy C might not take off as a vacation ranch. There was a developer there trying to convince Eli to sell. Scott Donaldson."

"He's a good-looking guy," Kaitlyn commented. "He asked me out when we were on a hospital committee in Sacramento."

"Did you go?" Marissa asked.

"No. I didn't date after my divorce, not until Adam."

"Do you know him?" Marissa asked Sara.

"The name sounds familiar. He might have been a guest at Raintree Winery's summer soiree. Are you interested in him?"

"Oh, no," Marissa said, shaking her head. "I just wondered if he's good at what he does, if he could convince Eli to sell."

"Do you know what the baby's dad wants?" Sara asked.

"Ty says he's committed to the Cozy C and to making it a success. He sounds sincere. And from what I've seen with him and Jordan...well, Jordan likes him. They related."

"So what's the conclusion, then?" Kaitlyn asked.

She was still figuring it out. But she knew one thing. "The conclusion is I have to do what's best for Jordan."

"You're a strong woman," Sara said.

If she went to live at the Cozy C, she'd have to be

strong enough to hold her own with a stubborn bull rider.

Could she hold her own with Ty? Could she control her own destiny—or would Ty's desire to be a dad trump all?

Chapter Five

The Thanksgiving food drive the following Saturday—
the weekend before Thanksgiving—was an important
event for The Mommy Club. Marissa donated some
canned goods, but more important than that, she was
helping prepare baskets and boxes for families in need.
This year, Sara had volunteered to children-sit for all
the volunteers.

Kaitlyn and her husband, Adam, had their heads together over a laptop. They were figuring out the best
route to deliver baskets to those families who couldn't
pick up their own or had no transportation to do so.
Adam's sister Tina, who was living at the guesthouse
at the winery, had left her baby in Sara's care while she
inserted coupons into the boxes that were already as-
sembled. The Mommy Club had helped her, too, and
she wanted to pay it forward.

They all did.

Sara's husband, Jase, carried in cartons of canned goods that had been left at drop-off points. Spotting Jase, Marissa thought about Scott Donaldson's request for her to take him on as a client and plan a Christmas event for him. If she could take on private clients like him, she wouldn't have to ask Jase for a raise.

She wasn't going to talk to Jase about that today. Everyone here was focused on what they were doing. She needed to wait for the right moment and do it the proper way so he didn't think she wanted to leave Raintree Winery. She appreciated so much everything he'd done for her.

Marissa had just labeled a box with the name Croft when she spied Ty entering the social hall. What was *he* doing here?

Ty canvased the room, appearing to absorb every bit of activity. He nodded to Jase as he came deeper in. After all, they *had* met.

Ty's gaze scanned the row of volunteers and stopped when he spotted *her*. Every one of his bootfalls toward her made her more aware of him. As he closed the distance between them, she felt the reactions in her body— from the shiver up her spine to the hummingbird heart rate of her pulse.

He had some kind of male pheromones that were more potent than any liquor or aphrodisiac she could imagine. One of the problems was, other women probably had the same reaction to him.

She spotted a couple of female heads turn. After all, he was the epitome of a rugged cowboy.

"Good morning," he said with a tip of his hat, and the smile that had led her into bed with him.

"Good morning to you, too. Did you come to help?"

"I can give a hand if you need it, but I don't belong to The Mommy Club." Again he gave her that smile that curled her toes.

"You could. Anyone who helps belongs to The Mommy Club." She gestured around the room. "All these baskets go to families who otherwise wouldn't have a Thanksgiving dinner."

His smile faded. "I know what it's like," he mumbled. "When my dad and I lived in Texas—" He stopped abruptly. She realized he hadn't meant to confide anything, at least not here.

"It doesn't matter," he said with a shake of his head. "You're doing good here."

"Why did you really come?"

"I remembered seeing this food drive on the Chamber of Commerce website. I went over to your place, and when you weren't home, I figured you might be here. I have great powers of deduction. You seem dedicated to this Mommy Club."

"I am, and your powers of deduction were right on. Why did you want to see me?"

"I need to know if you've come to a decision. I'd like to start making plans."

"Plans?"

"I want you to think about something, Marissa. My uncle has been alone for more years than I want to count. Some of that is my fault, and I want to rectify it. I haven't come back to the Cozy C often enough, and I regret it. So this year, I'd like to give Unc a real Thanksgiving. Imagine how much more special the holiday would be if you and Jordan were living there with us."

Sure, her finances were a consideration and Ty had

suggested she'd be better off by living at the Cozy C. Not having to parent alone was also a consideration. He'd mentioned that, too. And she didn't know if he was ever going to forgive her for keeping Jordan's birth from him, for keeping the first fourteen months of their baby's life a secret. She realized that to the bottom of her heart.

This new reason for her coming to live at the Cozy C jabbed at her emotions. Didn't everyone need family? Didn't everyone need a home?

Kaitlyn or Sara would include her in their celebration. There was no doubt about that. But Ty was Jordan's father. Eli was his great-uncle. Didn't that mean a whole lot?

Ty studied her with an intense regard. He didn't push. Although he didn't say "think about it," she knew that's what she'd do.

Instead, he said, "I'll help out for an hour or so. I was up before dawn working on the cabins but I'm waiting for supplies to roll in. I can help Jase Cramer unload that truck out there if you think that would be of help."

"It would," she assured him.

He nodded. "I'll let you know before I leave."

The subtext to that was easy. He'd like her decision before he left.

Marissa watched him walk away, thinking about that night they'd shared. How could she help it? That night he'd been so sexy, but caring, and interested in her pleasure, too. She'd seen that caring with Jordan. She had to admit she'd like to see more of it—with both her and her baby.

An hour later she'd finished up with one station of packing boxes and was about to take a break and visit with Jordan, who was happily sitting with Sara. They were looking at a book that made animal noises. He laughed every time he pushed a spot on the page and a moo or a hee-haw blared out.

Marissa went to him and bent down. "Are you having fun?"

He looked up at her, then went back to what he was doing.

"I can see you really miss me," she said with a laugh.

"He was watching you. He knew exactly where you were," Sara assured her.

And Marissa had known exactly where Ty was as well as Jordan.

After unloading the truck with Jase, he'd gone on to help sort the boxes. Now he came over to Marissa and Jordan.

She introduced him to Sara, and Sara gave Marissa a knowing look.

Ty took Marissa's elbow. His clasp was light, but the expression in his eyes wasn't. "Can we talk a few minutes?" he asked. "I'm getting ready to leave."

They stepped over to a corner of the room where the volunteers weren't working, where the kids weren't playing. He didn't have to ask her the question that was obviously on his mind.

"I thought about everything you said," she told him before he could speak.

He tipped his Stetson up with his forefinger and gave her a perusal that seemed to see deep inside of her. "And?" he prompted.

"You don't know exactly what's going to happen with the Cozy C. I don't know if living with you will work out. But I would like to move out of my apartment into something new. I can come stay with you temporarily and we can see if the arrangement works. In the meantime, I'll look for a new place in case I need it."

"In case our arrangement doesn't work," he said with a frown.

"Or…in case your uncle decides to sell the Cozy C."

"That's not going to happen," Ty growled.

But Marissa countered, "You could receive an offer neither of you could refuse."

Ty had started to shake his head, but Marissa held up her hand. "This will give us time, Ty, to see if we can parent together. Is that okay with you?"

"Who knew you could be a negotiator," he responded with a grimace. But then he looked toward Jordan and nodded. "We'll make it work, and we'll give Jordan a holiday that will give him a sense of family."

Marissa knew a holiday could be emotion-packed, and not all of the emotions were pleasant ones. But Ty wanted to make good memories, and so did she.

Thanksgiving, here we come.

On Monday morning, Marissa felt a bit nervous as she approached Jase in his office. At his desk, in a high-backed burgundy leather swivel chair, he turned his attention from his computer monitor to her.

"I'd like to talk to you for a few minutes," she said. "Do you have time?"

"Sure, I have time. Is there a problem with one of the clients…their orders?"

"No, nothing like that."

He motioned to the chair in front of his desk. "Have a seat."

She did and wiped her palms on her slacks. She

wasn't exactly sure how to go about this, but she figured it was best if she simply told Jase what had happened—on more than one front.

"Someone approached me about planning an event for him."

Jase's brows arched. "Who?"

"Scott Donaldson, the real estate developer. I wondered if you'd mind if I take on an outside job."

"I've run into Scott now and then," he said, studying her. After a silent lull, he went on, "Tell me, are you happy here at Raintree Winery?"

"Oh, yes, I am. But...I can use the extra money."

Jase looked thoughtful for a moment. "I can offer you a raise." He mentioned a figure. "I certainly want to keep you here. But I also don't want to hold you back. Are you thinking about going out on your own with an event-planning business?"

"No, nothing like that. At least not now."

"You're a valuable employee, Marissa, and I don't want to lose you. If you feel you need to take on extra work for whatever reason, I don't object."

"It won't affect my work here. But something else might."

Now Jase looked concerned.

"You've met Ty Conroy... He's Jordan's dad. He wants to try parenting...together...at the Cozy C."

Jase's brows creased. "I'm not going to interfere in your personal life, Marissa, but that's a plunge into something serious."

"Don't I know it. But with the holidays and all, it might be a good thing for everyone. So I told Ty I'd move in temporarily. Can I have a day off this week—tomorrow or Wednesday?"

Jase thought about it. "You're so efficient we're caught up for Thanksgiving. You can take the week. Next week we'll deal with the Christmas orders rush."

"Are you sure?"

"I'm positive. Moving into the Cozy C with a baby is going to be an adjustment. You'll need the time."

"Thank you," she said gratefully.

"No thanks necessary. You often put in extra hours for me and don't add them to your time sheet. Don't think I don't notice." He paused, then asked, "What if living at the ranch doesn't work out?"

"I'll look for another available apartment. If living at the ranch doesn't work out, with a raise and an outside project or two, I can afford to live someplace better."

Jase nodded. "So this isn't an impulsive decision."

"No, I don't make those anymore." She hadn't made an impulsive decision since the night she'd slept with Ty Conroy. She knew better now. Consequences and a sense of responsibility had taught her that she needed to plan.

That's exactly what she was doing.

Ty was ready for moving day on Tuesday. At least he thought he was until he'd showed up at Marissa's apartment with his truck and laid eyes on her again. Seeing her in jeans and a T-shirt with her hair tied back in a ponytail, he was hard-pressed to keep his focus on getting her furniture into that truck.

He had to focus, however, when Jase Cramer pulled into the parking lot in front of the apartment.

Marissa told Ty, "He offered to help and I accepted."

Ty knew Marissa had her support network and he

couldn't interfere in that. He didn't want to interfere in that. He was just wondering how he fit in.

Marissa really didn't have that much to move. Ty had emptied out the one bedroom used for storage at the ranch house. He'd wanted Marissa to be comfortable and feel at home, so her bedroom set would go in there. They'd put Jordan's crib in one of the smaller bedrooms.

By afternoon, they were all moved in at the Cozy C. Extra pieces, like Marissa's slip-covered couch, had been stowed in one of the outside storage sheds.

As Ty made sure the mattress was sitting on the bed correctly in Marissa's bedroom, Jase appeared with a white milk glass hobnail lamp and set it on the nightstand. He studied Ty a moment, and then said, "Marissa's a good friend." He looked around the bedroom. "This bedroom suite is the one thing she inherited from her mother, and it means a lot to her."

Ty hadn't known that and he wished he had. But he and Marissa hadn't had any long sit-down conversations since they'd spotted each other at the physical therapy center. Everything to date had been about Jordan. Ty figured Marissa was using that as a defensive maneuver. Maybe *he* was, too.

"I know Marissa has made a life for herself," Ty said. "I want to do the same thing."

"It's a different life than you've known." Jase plugged in the lamp and glanced over his shoulder at Ty.

"Yeah, it sure is. But I intend to make this vacation ranch venture a success. I'm also going to learn how to be a dad, a good one. And I know there are responsibilities that go with it."

"And what about Marissa? How does she fit into your life? Just as the mother of your son?"

"I'm not sure that's any of your business," Ty said pointedly.

But Jase didn't get ruffled. "You don't know how she fits in, do you?" he asked.

"Everything's a bit up in the air right now," Ty admitted.

Instead of warning Ty away from Marissa, as Ty thought Jase might, the former photojournalist said, "When I first met Sara, she was married with a two-year-old. She was my physical therapist, and I'd come through a hard time. The next time we came in contact, she was a widow, a single mom with a four-year-old. She had to put Amy first. We had to feel our way carefully until, well, I guess we couldn't be careful any longer." He hesitated a second, then said, "I guess what I'm trying to say is that this trial period with Marissa is probably a good thing…for both of you."

Ty wasn't sure what to say to that so he just nodded. "I'm not expecting too much, or expecting too little. We'll just see how it goes."

The two men left the bedroom then, and Ty almost felt like an alien on a strange planet. One day he was riding bulls, driving from state to state, winning championship purses. The next he was in a hospital room in Houston, looking at a recovery that was going to take months, if not longer. Now he was in his uncle's ranch house, and the woman he was strongly attracted to would be sleeping in the bedroom next door. Did fate have a sense of humor or what?

It was late afternoon when Ty stood with Marissa in Jordan's room. The baby had fallen asleep downstairs and Ty had carried him up to his crib.

"He might be up late tonight," Marissa warned. "If this is a late nap—"

"It doesn't matter."

She eyed Ty cautiously. "Babies often wake up in the middle of the night—maybe two, three times. I never know. Jordan's usually a good sleeper, but in a strange place, I don't know what will happen."

"If he wakes up and you think he's scared, come get me. I can always take the crib down and put it up in your room."

Marissa wasn't sure what to think of this Ty. She'd always thought of him as fun. Maybe she just hadn't looked for any deeper qualities. Or, on the other hand, maybe she'd sensed them all along.

"I'd like to hang decals on his walls. Maybe of horses. I don't have to make a nail hole or anything."

"Whatever you want to do. Unc and I won't mind a few holes if you want to hang pictures. More than anything, Marissa, I want you and Jordan to feel at home."

At home. How long had it been since she'd really had a home? Ever since her mom died, she'd felt as if she'd lost her roots. Ty didn't realize that what he was offering her was awfully tempting. But they had a lot of bridges to cross before she could even think about staying here permanently. And if she did, in what capacity?

"Can we talk a minute?" she asked.

"Sure. Your room?"

She'd already made up her room and she supposed that was as good an idea as any. She nodded, expecting Ty to precede her out. He didn't. He stayed by Jordan's crib, resting his thumb over the little boy's forehead. There was an expression on Ty's face she'd never seen before. Was that longing? Longing for home and family?

As she entered her room, she paused at the dresser. She always gravitated toward it. She could remember her mom standing in front of it. She'd laid a crocheted scarf there that her grandmother had made. A comb and brush and a framed photo of Jordan sat to one side. On the other side, she'd positioned a glass perfume bottle. It was pink with gold leaf squiggles and a painted white flower. It was a treasured memento.

Ty came in behind her and met her eyes in the mirror. "What's that?" he asked.

"It holds perfume," she said with a little catch in her voice. "My grandma gave it to my mom for her birthday one year."

"You like pretty things."

Marissa quickly shook her head. "I like memories. When I take off the stopper, I can still smell the scent of her perfume. It takes me back. It helps me feel like she's still watching over me—like both of them are."

Ty didn't seem to know what to say to that. But then he said, "It's tough losing a parent. No matter how it happens."

Marissa was ready to go deeper into that subject for his sake as well as hers when he changed the course of the conversation. She noticed that whenever they got a little too personal, he did that with topics he didn't want to talk about.

"What did you want to speak to me about?" he asked.

"I need to feel as if I'm useful while I'm here. After all, you're giving me room and board."

His brow furrowed. "This isn't about room and board. You're Jordan's mom. You don't have to do anything while you're here."

"I don't want to feel beholden, so just listen to me, okay?"

"Okay," he agreed. "Shoot."

"I can cook. I'd like to help out with meals."

Ty thought that over, then he nodded. "I'm sure Unc would appreciate that, and I would, too."

"And I want to help out with anything else that needs to be done. You said something about staining trim work at the cabins. I can do that."

This time Ty wasn't so quick to answer. "Maybe you can. But I don't know if I want you doing that. Let me think about it."

She would have moved away then but he took her arm, and when he did, she remembered the feel of his hands on her body, the way his kisses lifted her higher than she'd ever been lifted before.

His voice was low and gruff when he said, "This is going to work out, Marissa."

When she looked into those blue eyes of his, she could almost believe him.

When she looked into those blue eyes of his, she wanted to be held in his arms.

As if he'd read her thoughts, he folded one arm around her and he lifted her chin with his thumb. "We were magic that night," he said.

Had they been magic? Or had she felt too alone to *be* alone? Had Ty's sense of humor and sexy appeal wrapped itself around her as his arm was now? She could step back, step away, leave the room. But, oh, how she didn't want to. His arm around her, his thumb on her chin was just a taste of what they'd had that night.

She knew what was going to happen. After all, ever since they'd made love, she'd wondered how she'd feel if he kissed her again. She wondered how she'd feel if he touched her again. And now here he was doing it.

As his lips took hers, she remembered another way she'd felt that night—as if she belonged to him. Now as his tongue slid into her mouth, as he explored her, pulled her closer, touched her cheek so sensually she wanted to cry, she kissed him back. Not only did she kiss him back, she took hold of his shoulders, felt the male strength there and reacted like a woman who'd been hungry for a man's kiss for much too long.

"Marissa," he whispered, breaking the kiss, trailing his lips down her neck. He stopped to say, "This is right. You know it is."

Although she felt almost drugged by Ty's sexual appeal, by his warm touch, by his male scent, she was aware of the bed too, only about a foot away. She was aware of her mother's furniture in a strange house. But most of all, her motherly instincts kicked in, and she was totally aware of Jordan only about fifteen feet away. She might want to drown in Ty's kiss, but she knew better than to let him take it further than that. She knew better than to let herself take it further than that.

She shook her head and pushed away, breaking their contact but unable to break that wild connection.

She kept shaking her head and said, "No, we can't kiss and…" She threw her hands up in frustration. "And do any more than that, because I came here for Jordan's sake. We have a lot to figure out, and I'm not going to let a kiss from you muddle my thinking."

When she'd started speaking, he'd looked a little defensive. But now a smile twitched up the corner of his mouth. "My kisses muddle your thinking?"

"You know they do. I wouldn't have slept with you

if they didn't." She hadn't wanted to say it that bluntly, but that was the gist of what had happened.

"You think that night was just about kisses?" he asked more seriously now.

"Maybe not," she confessed. "But you're starting a new venture, and I'm trying to get used to the fact that you're in my life now. And in Jordan's. So let's just concentrate on that."

"It's hard to do," he muttered, "when you look so darn pretty, and every time I turn around, I can smell your shampoo."

"Do you want me to change shampoos?" She was teasing because she wanted to keep the atmosphere between them light if she could.

"No, I don't want you to change shampoos. I like it. But if I look at you as if I want to kiss you, I probably do." He headed toward the door. "Unc is making his favorite chili for supper. Is that okay with you?"

"Does he use hot sauce?" she asked.

"He does."

"If I could take a bit of it out before he puts the hot sauce in, I can give some to Jordan."

"Good idea. See, this is working out already."

She rolled her eyes as he left the room. Working out? They'd just have to see about that.

Late Wednesday morning, the oven timer went off while Marissa was mentally reviewing the preparations for Thanksgiving dinner the next day. She'd given Ty a shopping list last night and he'd bought everything on it, including a turkey so big he'd probably have to help her lift it into the oven.

They hadn't been around each other much since that

kiss. He was respecting her wishes and she was trying to keep out of his way.

In his play saucer, Jordan happily spoke gibberish as Eli came into the kitchen. Earlier he'd said he was going to muck out a few stalls while Ty was at physical therapy.

As he washed his hands at that new kitchen sink, he grumbled about it. "What a faucet! As if I don't have the strength to turn one on. And that new smartphone that Ty got me...what happened to just using a phone to talk to someone? What next?"

She had to admit she liked Eli. Oh, he was gruff sometimes, but he was honest and they seemed to understand each other.

He glanced at the four pumpkin pies already cooling on the table. "I thought I heard the timer go off on my way in."

"You did. Can you watch Jordan for a couple of seconds until I take these last two pies out of the oven?"

"Sure."

He went over to the little boy and said, "Mom is making us something good to eat, but I don't think we're going to need all of them."

She laughed as she opened the oven door. "Two of them are for us. The other four will go to the community center. Sara Cramer's going to pick them up later. They're serving dinner there for anyone who won't have food on the table for Thanksgiving."

As she placed one pie and then the other on cooling racks on the table, Eli said, "That could have been me if it weren't for Ty. But I would have been too proud to go."

"Even if your stomach was empty?" she asked. "I know what that's like, too, Mr. Conroy. My mom and

I had some rough times. But she always did what was best for me. She was a proud woman, but she often accepted handouts so I wouldn't go hungry. I respected her for that."

"Sometimes women do that better than men," Eli admitted. Then he said, "If you're going to live here, you can't keep calling me Mr. Conroy. How about trying out Eli?"

"I can do that, Eli," she said easily, happy that he'd asked her to.

Eli had placed his foot on the bottom rung of Jordan's saucer to keep him from walking and spinning his wheels. But now Jordan started to jump up and down and move side to side. He wanted to go.

Eli laughed. "I'd forgotten what it was like to have a young'un around."

"Not too much noise?" she asked.

"Nah. I didn't hear him at all last night. But then my rooms are pretty far from his. Did he sleep okay?"

"He has his own crib to sleep in, and his Humpty Dumpty night-light. He seems satisfied."

"Ty put him to bed last night, didn't he?" Eli sounded kind of proud when he said it.

"Yes, he did. Jordan likes the sound of his voice. I heard Ty telling him about the clowns at the rodeo before he went to sleep."

"So you think this is going to work out?" Eli asked her bluntly.

She answered just as bluntly. "It's too soon to tell."

Eli was thinking that over when they heard a truck rumble down the lane and park. It was Ty's truck. Marissa already knew the sound of the engine.

Moments later, Ty was coming up the steps in the

back and into the kitchen. But when Marissa saw him, he looked worn-out, and he was leaning heavily on his cane. She turned back to the pies and rearranged them on the table, figuring he wouldn't want her glimpsing his pain.

Obviously Eli wasn't keeping quiet. "How was PT?"

Without a word, Ty went to the freezer and took out an ice pack. "PT came and it went," he said, then he disappeared into the living room.

Eli exchanged a glance with Marissa. "I'll watch the baby if you want to check on him."

Eli's concern was obvious, and Marissa was concerned about Ty, too. Did he always come back from a physical therapy session looking as if he'd ridden in three rodeos?

"Thanks," she said to Eli. She ruffled Jordan's hair as she passed him.

She found Ty seated in a corduroy armchair, staring out the window. He had his leg propped up on the large hassock, the ice pack balanced there.

She sat on the space beside his foot and waited until he looked at her.

"What?" he asked in a low voice that said he didn't want to talk about anything.

"What's wrong?" she asked. "Rough physical therapy session?"

"I worked the muscles too hard and I strained one of them."

"Aw, Ty."

"I don't need your pity."

He shifted in the chair as if he were going to stand, but she moved closer so he couldn't and he stayed seated.

But he scowled. "I don't need a pep talk, either."

"You're impatient about recovery," she guessed.

"You're right—I am. It's been almost five gosh-darn months. Yeah, I'm back on a horse, but I'm using a mounting block. And a special saddle that's easier on the knee. Cripes," he muttered.

She didn't know how to help him. "You're too impatient. Your body will find its own pace. You're young and strong, Ty. You'll recover but it's going to take time. You're putting the effort in, but recovery takes more than effort."

"How do you know so much?"

"I work with Jase. He talks about what he went through after he got shot in Kenya and came back home to recuperate. It wasn't easy for him, either. Maybe you should talk to him about it."

"I read about that online. He was shot by a gang of bandits when he was photographing children in a refugee camp, right?"

"Yep. Something he couldn't have foreseen, either. He didn't want to come back to his father's winery, but now he can't imagine being anywhere else."

"I suppose there's a message in that."

"Maybe."

Ty had leaned forward as they were talking, and her knee was practically brushing his thigh. Serious conversation had revved up emotion between them, and they could both feel it. Their kiss yesterday practically flashed like a movie streaming in front of their eyes.

Marissa licked suddenly dry lips.

Ty groaned and leaned forward a little more. "You are the most tempting woman—"

The sound of Ty's cell phone buzzing broke the electric current sizzling between them. With a sigh and a quick sly smile, Ty reached in his pocket for his phone. "Saved by the proverbial bell," he remarked.

She moved back on the hassock to put a little distance between them.

"Hi, Clint," he said into his phone. "It's good to hear from you."

Marissa would have gotten up to leave, but Ty held up a finger. He wanted her to stay. What now?

"Sure, that's great that you'll be here tomorrow. Hold on a minute." He put the phone on Mute and looked up at Marissa.

"Clint said he'll be getting in in the early hours of the morning. He'll be staying in the bunkhouse. But I wanted to check with you before I invited him for Thanksgiving dinner. Would that be okay?"

"We have more than enough food," she said with a smile, remembering Ty had said Clint was an old friend.

Ty turned his attention back to the phone and asked Clint, "You will have Thanksgiving dinner with us tomorrow, won't you?"

Marissa wondered how one of Ty's rodeo friends was going to enter into the mix. Would this Clint bring back memories of rodeo escapades Ty couldn't shake? Or would he be a buffer between her and Ty and actually make things easier between them?

Maybe a holiday dinner would reveal a bit of the future. Or maybe it would remind Ty of the past that he'd like to have back.

Chapter Six

On Thanksgiving Day, Marissa had thought she had everything under control. But now she was mashing the potatoes, the green beans were finished and had to be removed from the heat, and the turkey had to be carved.

Suddenly, there Ty was at her elbow, watching her mash the potatoes.

"Jordan's in good hands," he said. "Clint and Eli are playing peekaboo with him. Do you need help out here?"

"Yes, I do," she said with some relief. "Can you drain the beans and add butter? Then we'll cover them. And if you could take the turkey out—"

He laid a hand on her shoulder. "Whoa. We'll get it all done."

When she glanced up at him, she felt a thrill that had no place in her stomach while she was mashing potatoes. Her hunger should be for this Thanksgiving Day meal, nothing else. Yet when Ty looked at her like that…

"Since kissing you again right now would interrupt meal preparations," he said in a low voice, "I'll find dishes for the green beans and stuffing, then I'll get to that turkey."

Taking a deep breath and swallowing hard, she concentrated on making sure the potatoes were seasoned just right.

An eruption of laughter emanated from the living room.

After Ty took the turkey from the oven, he asked Marissa, "What do you think of Clint?"

She'd only talked to him briefly when Ty had introduced her this morning. Clint Detwiler was tall, lanky and about forty-five. He was a rugged-looking guy with a scar on his face and a tattoo on his arm.

"I don't know yet," she said honestly, her voice lowered. "Did he settle in at the bunkhouse all right?"

"He's used to bunkhouses and sleeping in a room with a couple of other guys."

"Are you hiring on anyone else?"

"Another hand is starting on Monday morning. I made a good deal with him for room and board."

"So everything's coming together," Marissa said.

"Yes, it is. All we need now are tourists lining up at our door come the new year."

Marissa was totally aware of Ty as he worked beside her. She pulled a salad from the refrigerator and garnished it with cherry tomatoes. Ty reached around her for the hand towel on the counter and she held her breath and kept herself from leaning into him. But as he pulled the towel from the counter, she thought she felt him release a long breath.

The atmosphere between them was heavy with desire and expectation as she finished putting Thanksgiving dinner on the table. Eli stood to say grace, and even Jordan seemed to grasp the importance of the moment because he stayed quiet.

With his head bowed, Eli said gruffly, "Never expected this group gathered around this table today. But I give thanks for it—for my nephew, my great-nephew, Jordan's mom and somebody to help us with all the work here. Thanks too for the food. Amen."

Ty was seated next to Marissa. He asked, "What's Jordan having?"

"I'll smash up bits of turkey and beans in with the mashed potatoes. He's going to make a mess, but he'll like it."

Clint glanced at Marissa then back at Ty as if he didn't know what to make of the whole situation. "Are you going to teach the little one to ride?" he asked Ty with a smile.

"He started out by touching Goldie's nose. I might set him in a saddle to see what he thinks about it one of these days."

At Marissa's surprised look, Ty said, "I would keep my hands on him good and strong, of course."

Again Clint looked from one to the other. "Do you remember that day Ted Barstow brought his five-year-old to the barrel racing competition? That little boy wanted to get on a horse in the worst way."

That memory sparked others, and soon the conversation was about rodeo shenanigans and the riders they'd known.

At a lull, Marissa asked Clint, "Are you really retiring from the circuit?"

Clint nodded. "Too many aches and pains to ride

right. I don't want to give it up any more than Ty wants to, but there comes a time. Watching what happened to him made me realize you never know what will happen next. Being on a ranch, taking people on trail rides, showing them this beautiful country seems like a good way to spend my life now."

She nodded, liking the sincerity in his voice.

"What are you going to do about grub for the guests?" Clint asked Ty.

"I found an out-of-work cook in town. He'll be ready to start for us when I need him. I'm just hoping we have guests for him to feed."

The talk after that was about the marketing plans for the Cozy C. Over pie and coffee, Marissa started thinking up ideas of her own to promote the ranch. She'd share them with Ty when she got the chance.

She put Jordan in his play saucer while she cleared the table. The men paid him some attention while she stowed away the food.

She was at the refrigerator, hunkered down trying to fit everything in, when she heard Clint ask Ty in a low voice, "Have you heard from Darla?"

"Nope," Ty answered tersely, as if that was the end of the conversation.

Apparently it was, because nothing else was said on the subject.

But it was all Marissa could think of. Who was Darla?

Marissa didn't have a chance all day to ask Ty about the woman. Finally, when she put a sleeping Jordan down for the night, she hoped she'd have an opportunity. She was restless and didn't want to just go to her room. It was too early to sleep, and she wasn't in the mood to read. She heard sounds in the kitchen downstairs—a dish clattered and the silverware drawer jingled open. Ty hadn't turned in or couldn't sleep, either. Maybe she could find out if this Darla had been important in his life.

When she entered the kitchen, she saw that Ty had changed from a snap-button shirt and almost-new jeans to a black T-shirt and worn denims.

"I couldn't resist another piece of that pie," he said with a smile. "Clint took one along to the bunkhouse, too."

Before she'd put Jordan to bed, Clint had thanked her for making a great Thanksgiving dinner. She liked him, and what he'd had to say about settling down.

"I think he'll be good with your guests," she said honestly. "He's down-to-earth, friendly and if he knows his way around horses, what more could you want?"

"He's always been a good friend," Ty offered, slipping the piece of pie onto a plate and taking it to the table.

She followed him, but didn't give him a chance to sit down and make small talk. She wanted to get to the heart of the matter right now.

"Who's Darla?" she asked in an even tone, hoping nothing else escaped with the question except minor interest.

"Darla's not important," Ty said with a shrug.

"Apparently she was important enough for Clint to mention her."

Ty rolled his eyes. "I thought you were deep in the refrigerator and didn't hear."

"I heard."

"I told you, there wasn't anything to say. She was just another case of love-gone-wrong."

Marissa studied him and his closed expression. Ty didn't express emotion easily, but she was going to get to the bottom of this.

"You mean *love* gone wrong? Or do you mean *sex* gone wrong? Did you expect sex and she expected more?"

"I don't discuss what happened in private," he answered crisply. Then he turned the tables on her. "When we had sex, was *that* sex-gone-wrong?"

After trying to see into his heart and being unable to do it, she decided to give him the simple truth. "Right or wrong, having sex with you changed my life." She turned to go. "I'll see you in the morning. Bacon and eggs for breakfast?"

"Whatever you make will be just fine," he said.

That was the end of their discussion for now. But eventually she'd find out who Darla was and what she'd meant to Ty.

If he still had a romantic connection to someone— Marissa didn't like that idea at all.

Before the bacon and eggs, before Jordan roused, Marissa decided to talk to Ty about something else, and that subject wasn't Darla—though the woman was still on her to-be-discussed list. She waited until she heard Ty leave the bathroom, then she opened her door. Ty's jeans rode low, he was shirtless, and she caught the scent of shaving lotion. Oh, sure, she could have a discussion when he looked and smelled like *that*.

Keeping her voice low, she pointed to *his* bedroom this time. She didn't want to wake Jordan.

He nodded and they both stepped inside the door.

Ty's bedroom was Spartan. The bed was an antique, for sure. It was a beautiful oak that had changed color and become a rich russet with age. There were cannonballs on the footboard and two on the headboard. The sheets were rumpled, and she could see the bed had been covered with a simple cotton navy spread. There were no blinds at the windows or curtains. Who needed them out here? Ty had a view of trees and pastures and the fence line.

His dresser was empty save for his wallet and keys and a bit of change. The chest of drawers held no adornment. A belt and a pair of jeans lay over a straight-backed chair with a cane seat. She didn't know what was worse, staring at the bed or staring at Ty's broad chest with those wisps of hair that were so enticing.

"Why are you up so early?" Ty asked. "Did Jordan have you up?"

"No, he slept through the night. I wanted to talk to you."

He frowned and she wondered if he was expecting another question about Darla. That could wait. What she had in mind couldn't.

"Remember we talked about me helping out around here?"

"I remember," he said warily.

"Eli told me you intend to stain that trim work on the cabinets today. I'm going to take Jordan to Mommy Club day care and then I want to help."

"Marissa—"

"The cabins have decks that need to be stained, too. If you don't want me on the finish work, I can stain the deck while you and Clint do the rest. How hard can that be? There's nothing for me to mess up."

"You don't want to just hang around with Jordan today?"

"I always want to hang around with Jordan. But there's work to be done here, and if you want to be ready by January, you have a lot to accomplish. I imagine Clint would rather work with the horses, and you want to round up guests. Lets get the rest done and you can do that."

After a few beats of silence, he asked, "How about if I make you a deal."

Now she was the one who was wary. "What kind of deal?"

"I'll let you help today if you let me handle Jordan for an afternoon on my own."

She felt her throat tighten.

He suddenly had his hands on her shoulders, looking straight into her eyes. "Don't look so afraid, Marissa. It's not like I'm going to run away with him. I just want to prove to you that he and I can spend some guy time together without you watching over us. You watch every move I make with him. I need to have a little bit of freedom with my son."

There was just a bit of emphasis on the words *my son*.

Deep down, she'd known eventually Ty would ask for this time with Jordan, but she still wasn't prepared.

"You leave him with the babysitters at the day care center," Ty prompted.

"But they're trained with kids," she said.

"Maybe so. But I won't learn unless I'm with him, will I?"

"You have to promise me not to put him on a horse," she blurted out.

His lips twitched up and there was amusement in his eyes. "I promise. I'll let him pet Goldie and that's as far as we'll go."

"And what else will you do?" she asked, wondering if he knew anything about entertaining kids.

"He has a toy bin we can explore. And I saw those books he has that make animal sounds. We can always read. The point is, Marissa, you have to go spend a couple hours with friends or find something to do away from here. How about Sunday afternoon?"

"After church," she murmured.

"After church is fine."

"He takes a nap around three."

"After church till three. That sounds good to me."

He was still holding on to her, and she was so tempted to hold on to him. But if she did, her whole world could come crashing down around her if this didn't work out.

He leaned forward and brushed his lips across her forehead. It was just the slightest of kisses. Yet she felt it deeply. When she breathed in, she smelled his shaving soap. She smelled him.

"That bed isn't faraway and Jordan is still asleep," he murmured close to her ear.

He was tempting her, and the truth was she was so close to succumbing to the temptation. Good sense prevailed however as she laid her palm against his bare chest, feeling the heat, the tautness of his skin, the strength underneath.

"Eli will be up soon. I'll get breakfast started if you look in on Jordan before you come down."

"I'll look in on Jordan," he agreed, a knowing look in his eyes.

He knew she was fighting her attraction to him. He knew she wanted to find passion in his arms again. But that wasn't on her to-do list right now. Getting the Cozy C shipshape for January was. Once the Cozy C was up and running, she'd be able to tell just how committed Ty was to it and to staying here in Fawn Grove.

Where Marissa thought she'd be staining the decks and essentially be alone doing it, she was wrong. Ty asked Clint to see to the decks, explaining a tricky sprayer was involved. He felt Clint could handle the large machine a little easier than she could.

So that's how she ended up in the first guest cabin with Ty, working on the window sashing, plastic spread on the floor to catch any drips of stain. The tension between them had everything to do with almost kisses, and wants and desires they weren't meeting.

"I like the light wood tones in the cabins," she said to make conversation. "I like the warm feel the wood gives when you walk in here. Did you paint the interiors?"

"I had a hand in it."

The interior walls held a coat of rough plaster that was then painted a creamy yellow. With the lighter wood trim, the color added brightness to the interior.

They could hear the strokes of their brushes as they applied the stain. And maybe the sound of their thoughts. When they made eye contact, the room seemed to shake a bit.

Maybe she was just going crazy. Ty-crazy. "Do you have furniture picked out yet?" she asked, changing the subject to give herself something else to think about other than the man beside her.

He shifted to reach a longer expanse of the window frame. "I have some in mind that I saw at one of the furniture stores in town."

She dipped her brush into the stain. "If we went to the used furniture store, I'm sure we could find some good pieces at a decent price."

When he shrugged, his T-shirt molded to his upper arm muscles. "I didn't think I'd have time for that."

Staring at the trim work before her, rather than at him, she offered, "I wouldn't mind looking for you if you're not too particular about what you'd like."

Their gazes met again. "Not particular at all. Except I want it to be comfortable."

A half hour later they were working on the last window frame—together. As each of them painted up their own side, Ty asked, "So would you like to stay here if you were a tourist?"

She gave the cabin another once-over, even eyeing the small kitchen. "I would. It has everything I'd need— a bedroom, a sitting room and a place to cook. You know I was thinking—"

"Uh-oh," Ty said with a teasing tone. "That could be trouble."

She batted his arm and he grinned at her. "What were you thinking?" he prodded.

"I was just wondering if the Cozy C and Raintree Winery could do a promotion together. You could both benefit. We can offer a 10 percent reduced rate for Raintree Winery Club guests."

"Winery Club?"

"Yes. They receive a case of wine a month and have

access to events just for them. They're the cream of the crop of our customers, live across the state and beyond. You could do the same thing. Have a sign-up for the Cozy C Vacation Club. Every year the members would get a discount. Guests who stay here would receive coupons for Raintree Winery wines. What do you think?"

He looked at her in a way that made dreams come alive again.

She had that feeling even more so when he said, "You're one smart woman, Marissa. Those ideas are good. I'll have to talk to Jase about them. I'll call him later and make an appointment. I can't stop in tomorrow. I'm going to a horse auction, but maybe Monday."

He laid his brush on top of the can of stain. "In fact, I was wondering. Would you like to come along? We can take Jordan."

"A restless baby and a horse auction might not go together well."

Ty shrugged. "It's nothing the two of us can't handle. There will be lots of sights and sounds and people. I think he'll be occupied with it all. We can take that stroller you said you have in your car."

A day away from the Cozy C with Ty. And Jordan. Sounded appealing. "I've never been to a horse auction."

"We're looking for two more horses we can use for trail rides. I'll need them to handle well for the guests to use them. The facility might even have hot dogs and burgers to whet our appetites, possibly ice cream."

Marissa laughed. "Now that's a meal Jordan probably can't refuse."

"But you can?"

Ty was leaning toward her, and she was leaning toward him. Working together like this, talking like this, made her feel close to him. Not quite as close as she felt that night after the wedding, but still—

"I'm going to kiss you, Marissa. Is that okay with you?"

She supposed he was telling her because if she really wanted to run away, she could. But she was still standing there, not even thinking of leaving. She was just drowning in his eyes and waiting to see what would happen next.

Next.

He bent to her slowly, letting them both savor what was going to happen. Then he brushed his lips across hers, so teasingly she practically moaned. She could feel his smile against her lips, and she realized he knew exactly what he was doing.

Her brush fell to the newspaper on the floor, and her arms went around his neck. He pulled her closer, and his kiss became possessive in a way the last one hadn't been. This one was deeper and longer and wetter. It told her he wanted to sleep with her again. It told her his body hungered for hers. It told her Ty was the sexiest man she'd ever known.

When he broke the kiss and leaned away, he said, "Your kisses always knock me for a loop. I think I'm going to be in control, and then something just happens."

His honesty touched her. "Tomorrow we'll have to behave while we're out in public. We wouldn't want to give anybody the wrong idea."

"And just what is the wrong idea?" he asked with a lifted brow. "We're living together. We have a son together."

"But we aren't together," she reminded him.

"Not in the way you mean," he said.

"Jordan deserves more than his parents being lovers. If that ends badly, he's the one who gets hurt."

She removed herself from Ty's embrace.

But Ty caught her wrist. "You will go with me tomorrow, won't you?"

This connection she had with Ty could go somewhere, or it might not. But the only way to find out was to be with him more often, to spend time with him off of the Cozy C.

However, when she said, "Yes, I'll go with you," she wondered if she wasn't making another mistake—like the one she'd made the night of her friend's wedding.

That evening Marissa had taken a shower, picked up Jordan from day care and was putting together a supper of leftovers when there was a knock on the front door.

Eli called from the living room, "I'll get it."

Marissa wondered who would be calling. Scott Donaldson again?

She heard Ty's bootfalls as he came down the stairs. He and Clint had wanted to finish the cabins and had worked late. But now he was freshly showered, too, and from the looks of it, he might have even shaved again.

They both looked toward the living room when they heard a woman's voice.

Ty said, "That's Hannah Johnson."

Marissa waited for further explanation and Ty smiled. "She's the neighbor I told you about. The one who often brings us food. She was bringing Eli food long before I came along. I think she's sweet on him."

They couldn't talk anymore then because Eli and

Hannah came into the kitchen. Eli was holding a casserole.

Marissa had heated gravy with pieces of turkey in it. The mixture was simmering. She'd warm up the mashed potatoes in the microwave as well as the stuffing and they could pour the turkey mixture over it.

Hannah looked at the dishes on the counter and the pot on the stove. She said, "I never imagined you'd be making Thanksgiving dinner. There's more turkey, stuffing and mashed potatoes in that casserole."

Since Eli didn't step in to guide the conversation, Ty did. He crossed to the corner of the kitchen where Jordan was playing with blocks and hefted him into his arms.

Then he crossed to Hannah. "Our situation has changed a little since you were here last. This is my son, Jordan, and his mom, Marissa. They're staying at the Cozy C now, and Marissa's a great cook."

Hannah beamed at Jordan. "Hey, little guy, aren't you a cutie? Will you come to me?" She held out her arms and she glanced at Marissa. "Do you mind?"

"No, I don't mind at all," she assured the woman, who had kind blue eyes, fluffy gray hair and a smile from ear to ear. She was a little plump and her cheeks were rosy.

"I'm Hannah Johnson," she said to Marissa as she took the baby. "Eli and I go way back."

Marissa looked to Eli for clarification while Hannah jiggled Jordan and cooed at him. He seemed happy enough in her arms.

Eli said, "We went to school together before everybody had cell phones."

Marissa couldn't help but laugh. Addressing Hannah, she assured her, "I'm sure we can use your casserole, too. These guys have big appetites. We'll probably finish up our leftovers today. They're going to have to fight over the last piece of pie tonight, too."

Now Hannah laughed. "I make pies, too. We'll have to compare notes sometime." Then Hannah looked over at Eli. "You'd think you'd let me know you have a grand-nephew."

"You would have found out when you come here to clean," Eli said.

"Do you still want me to do that?" Hannah wanted to know, looking again at Marissa.

"I work full-time," Marissa explained. "So if you clean for Eli that would be a help for all of us."

"No reason not to keep it the way it is," Eli mumbled, looking anywhere in the kitchen but at Hannah. Hannah, on the other hand, gazed at him adoringly.

Marissa wondered if the two had been high school crushes who'd gone their separate ways. She didn't have long to ponder it before Jordan reached out his arms to Marissa and she took him from Hannah.

Hannah said, "I'll be going. I don't want to interrupt your dinner. But if you ever need a babysitter, just give me a call. My son has never married, and I don't see babies on the horizon." She told Eli, "I'll be over on Tuesday as usual. You don't have to see me out."

As quick as she'd dropped into their lives, she was out the front door again.

Eli noted, "We might have to get someone younger to keep up with all this. We'll need someone to clean those guest cabins, too."

"You don't want Hannah coming around anymore?"

Marissa asked. "She seems like a fine woman. Aren't you interested?"

Ty gave her a warning look that said this was an area she probably shouldn't tread in. But if they were all going to be family, she had to know what was going on.

As Marissa lowered Jordan into his high chair, Eli sat at the table. "She *is* a good woman. She's been a widow about ten years. But I have nothing to offer her. I can't even pay my taxes."

"*Couldn't* pay them," Ty corrected him. "They're paid now."

"A woman likes security," Eli retorted. "I can't give it. Everything here is still uncertain. I sure as heck can't handle getting involved with a woman." He paused a moment, then added, "Even if I'd want to."

Marissa studied Ty, who didn't say anything. She wondered if he felt the same way. Was everything still too uncertain for him to be involved in anything more than an affair?

Could they both handle an affair?

The fact that she was even thinking about sleeping with Ty again scared the dust off her boots.

Chapter Seven

Marissa had gotten Jordan up before he was awake on Saturday morning and her son was in a cantankerous mood. She knew Ty wanted to get going to the auction so she hurried breakfast a little. No pancakes this morning, just bacon, eggs and toast.

"Ketchup or hot sauce?" she asked the two men as they took chairs at the table.

Ty used ketchup and Eli used hot sauce. It had become a pattern, and now Jordan wanted ketchup on his eggs, too. He banged his little fist on his tray and shot a gap-toothed grin at Ty.

Before Marissa could say, "Don't give him ketchup this morning, because he has a nice clean new shirt on," Ty spooned some on Jordan's dish beside his eggs. The little boy banged on his tray with his fist.

"He's grumpy when I get him up early," Marissa said.

"Not so different from a lot of cowboys I know," Ty joked.

"What are you going to bid on today?" Eli asked.

"I'm not sure. It depends on what I see."

"You might run into folks you used to know."

Marissa caught Eli's comment as a subtle warning. Ty would have a baby and a woman along. And just what would he say if anyone asked questions?

Suddenly, without warning, Jordan gripped his plate with both his little hands and flipped it over. Eggs, ketchup and a spoonful of applesauce Marissa had put on his plate flew all over him, the tray and the floor.

She, of course, had seen this happen before, but it was a bit startling for those who hadn't.

Eli muttered, "That little rascal."

Ty said in a firm voice, "Jordan!"

Marissa stared at Jordan and the mess, then looked at Ty. "Why don't you go to the auction by yourself? I don't want to make you late. This will take a while to clean up."

But Ty didn't seem overly worried. Rather, he seemed more concerned about teaching Jordan the right thing to do. He flipped the little boy's plate right side up. Then he put some of his eggs on Jordan's dish and scooped up a spoonful.

He stared at his son straight in the eye and said, "How about if we eat some of this instead of playing with it."

Marissa didn't know if it was the tone of Ty's voice or the way he was looking at Jordan, but Jordan didn't make a fuss. With ketchup and applesauce smeared all over his new shirt, he opened his mouth and he let Ty spoon the eggs in.

After another spoonful, Marissa asked, "How did

you do that? Usually after one of these little tantrums, he won't eat at all."

"It's a guy thing," Ty said, readying another spoonful. "We understand each other, don't we, son?"

She got his drift and actually she was quite impressed with it. He wasn't going to let a baby run roughshod over him. She guessed she let Jordan have his way sometimes because she felt guilty being the only parent. She felt guilty that she couldn't give Jordan all the things she wanted to give him.

"He'll be a tyrant by two if you give him too much slack," Ty advised her. But then he glanced at her. "Sorry, I don't mean to give you advice. I know nothing about kids. But I know something about horses, and I'm not sure they're too much different."

At that she laughed. "Are you sure you don't want to get going?"

He shook his head and checked his watch. "We're good. I'll clean up down here while you change him. We'll be on the road in half an hour."

Eli had watched it all with interest. Now he winked at his nephew as if to say, "You handled that well."

Yes, Ty had. Is this the kind of everyday dad he'd be? Or was he putting on a good front for her benefit? She knew she didn't trust easily. Because of her father's example, she didn't trust men to stay, or to be consistent or committed.

But handling a baby at a horse auction could try the patience of a saint. She couldn't wait to see how Ty would handle that.

In Ty's crew cab truck with a double horse trailer behind, Marissa glanced at him often. Jordan napped once they were on the road and she found herself actually relaxing.

"They auction the tack first," he said as they approached Crossbow Ranch where the auction would take place. "So we'll be there in plenty of time for the horses."

"I'm surprised you brought the trailer when you don't know if you're going to buy a horse."

"Oh, I'm going to buy a horse. It's just a matter of which one or ones. I saw the list and there are several possibilities."

"So this isn't like a horse rescue auction?"

"No. But there is one of those farther north, and I might consider it in the spring. This is a private consignment auction. The horses have already been quarantined and vetted by a vet so I won't have to keep them separated from the others for three weeks, though I will for a little while to give them a chance to get adjusted."

Marissa glanced over her shoulder into the backseat at Jordan. He was awake again and seemed happy enough to be riding along, playing with the keys attached to his car seat. Without ketchup on his face or shirt, and in a more placid mood, he was a congenial baby once more. She just hoped that lasted throughout the day.

After they parked, Ty put Jordan in his stroller and started pushing him toward an outbuilding.

"We have to check in at the office to get a bidding number," he explained.

"Do they take credit cards?" she joked.

"They do. They even do phone sales. If you're interested in a horse and can't be here, you can get in on the bidding by phone. Even horse auctions are high-tech now. Crossbow Ranch even streams the auction on its website."

After they checked in, they headed toward an indoor arena.

"Do you get to ride a horse before you buy it?"

"You can during the presale. That's what the morning hours are for."

She eyed him quizzically. "But you're not."

"I saw a video sent from the owners on the horses I'm interested in. Their teenagers were riding the two I'll bid on. There are pens inside where I can check them out, too. I don't need to ride a horse to get a good idea of its constitution or behavior."

Was that it? Or did he not want to use a mounting block in a public place such as this? Did he not want to admit he maybe couldn't do some of the things he once did?

She wasn't sure if that was the reason, but she trusted Ty had been around horses long enough to know what he wanted.

She wheeled Jordan in and out of groups of people—men in boots and Stetsons, women in jeans and just as sturdy boots. When they stopped at one of the pens, Ty took out his smartphone and checked something on it. Then he studied a bay gelding with a black forelock. The horse had a number on its flank—fifty-three. Ty's gaze seemed to study every bit of the horse's constitution.

When he clicked his tongue against his teeth and the horse trotted over, Ty ran his hand down the horse's neck.

Jordan burbled from his stroller seat and Ty cast a glance down at him. "Do you like this one?"

When Jordan answered with a toothy grin, Ty bent

down to him. "Even if your mom makes us wait until you're three, you're going to be a great rider."

Just then an older man, possibly Eli's age, came up beside Ty. "Didn't know you had a young'un," the older man said.

Ty rose to his feet. "Hi, Bart. Yes, I do. This is Jordan."

But before Bart could make another comment, Ty nodded to another pen. "You know Whitmore Stables. What do you think about that pregnant mare?"

All of their gazes swung to a pretty gray who was obviously pregnant.

Bart studied the horse for a few moments. "Whitmore has a good reputation. I'd go for it. You'll get two for one."

Bart took another look at Jordan, then at Marissa, as he walked away but didn't say anything else.

"You didn't introduce me," Marissa said. She wasn't offended; she just wondered why.

"I didn't want any more questions. Bart can be kind of nosy—and a gossip. The fact that I'm a dad will get around to all these folks pretty quickly."

Marissa nodded to the horse. "I'm surprised you'd want the additional care of a pregnant mare, especially right now."

"I have choices," he said. "I can either sell the foal or keep it and train it. I figure if the Cozy C is going to be a vacation ranch, that experience isn't just about trail rides and staying overnight in the cabins. It's about the whole ranch life experience. A foal can add to that spirit."

"You've really put a lot of thought into this," she acknowledged.

"Wouldn't you?"

If it was going to be her future, she would. If it was more than a passing fancy, she would.

As Ty gazed into her eyes, everybody and everything around them seemed to drop away. Could he be a solid, stable family man? And even if he was, and even if she was attracted to him, and she was, could they have a future?

He leaned closer to her and murmured in her ear, "Stop thinking so much, Marissa. Too much thinking and you'll lose what's going on right now." He nodded to Jordan, who seemed entranced by the line at the food cart, the horses in the pens, the people milling around.

"He doesn't seem intimidated by any of it."

"That's because he's my son."

She noticed how Ty always said those words with pride—and maybe even with love.

When the tack portion of the auction began, Ty bid on several saddles and won two bids. He seemed to know when to stop and when to push higher. At one point he asked if she'd be okay while he went to discuss one of the horses with the owner.

"Of course I'll be okay."

"New place, new situation," he said with a quirk of his brow.

"I've learned to be adaptable," she quipped.

He gave her one of those long probing looks and she wondered what he saw. The girl he'd made love with, or the woman and mom she'd become?

She took in the sights and sounds, every once in a while glancing at Ty's broad back, his tall stature, his serious expression as he spoke to a small wiry man who looked as if he could have been a jockey. Ty was in his element here—at home.

However, after he came back to stand with her, to watch more horses paraded before them, a balding, paunchy man approached them. "When are you going back to rodeoing?" the man asked Ty. "I haven't seen you on the cowboy channel."

A stoic expression crossed Ty's face. "Mr. Carrington, meet Marissa Lopez. And this is my son, Jordan."

"So you're a family man now? Isn't that kind of tough when you're never home? But it looks like you were home at some point for some R & R." He nodded to Jordan.

Marissa felt her cheeks grow red. "It's good to meet you, Mr. Carrington," she said with a bit of wryness to her tone.

"It's good to meet you, too."

So there was no misunderstanding, Ty said tersely, "I won't to be returning to the rodeo circuit."

Carrington asked, "So that accident you had was worse than everybody thought?"

"Knee replacement," Ty answered, as if he didn't even want to think about it.

Carrington nodded. "That doesn't mean you have to be out of the rodeo business, though."

Marissa wondered what *that* meant.

When Ty didn't comment, the older man went on to say, "I suppose it's better to quit than to end up as your father did. That night you took a spill, it could have been fatal."

"Yes, it could have," Ty agreed. Even though Ty had always known the danger, she was certain that if he hadn't taken that spill, he'd still be bull riding.

When the man walked away, Ty's attention returned

to the auction, but Marissa wondered what he was thinking. Did regret lurk behind those eyes?

After Ty bid and won his second horse, the pregnant gray, he made arrangements to have both horses transferred to his trailer so they could drive home.

Taking a few minutes while all the paperwork was handled and the horses readied, they bought fries and burgers and barbecued beans and carried them to a picnic table under a live oak. They were later than most having their lunch, and not many folks lingered there.

Marissa took Jordan's lunch from an insulated pouch inside the diaper bag. She fed him that but she also dipped a fry in ketchup and gave him a little bite. He grinned at her and clapped his hands.

"I'm glad to see you're not an all-organic parent," Ty said with a grin. "He'd miss out on fun foods."

"I want him to eat healthy, but a treat now and then doesn't hurt. I guess parenting is all about knowing when to draw the line and when not to."

Since they were fairly alone and Jordan was occupied with the spinning beads on his stroller, and since she and Ty had been getting along fairly well, she let her arm rest against his as she asked, "What was it like growing up with your uncle?"

Ty was quiet for a long moment. Then he asked, "Do you mean before or after my dad was killed?"

"Before," she said.

"It was fine," he responded as if that was enough of an explanation.

But she gently clasped his forearm, seeing that his life hadn't been fine.

"Tell me about it," she suggested. "You were living with your uncle before your dad died?"

"We were living in Texas when my mom left my dad and me, when his rodeo winnings were practically non-existent. After she left, Dad moved us to live with Uncle Eli. For a while he worked on the ranch beside Unc, but then the circuit called him again. He just couldn't leave it, couldn't get the taste for sawdust out of his head. Once he was back to bull riding, he hardly ever came home. I guess if he did, he'd be reminded he had a son and responsibility. He'd never been good at responsibility. So I had two parents who didn't think a kid was so important. They didn't understand that everything they did mattered."

Ty turned toward Marissa, his knee bumping hers, his body sliding closer to hers, his blue eyes mesmerizing her. "I know what it's like not to have parents who care. I know what it's like to think I was the one who did something wrong, and that's why they left. So believe me, I understand what I need to do with Jordan. I understand that every decision I make affects him."

Ty seemed so passionate about that, just as passionate as he was about other things. Just like his kisses. Each of his kisses burned passion into her. Each of his touches reminded her what bliss could be.

He leaned even closer. "I'd kiss you right now if I didn't want to start another chain of gossip around here."

"I think they're already gossiping," Marissa said. "After all, you told everyone you have a son."

Ty smiled. "Yes, I did, didn't I? Well, then, I guess everyone already knows I'm attracted to the little boy's mother."

With that, he leaned in. The brim of his Stetson gave them an iota of privacy. Enough privacy that he took a deep, long, fervent kiss. When it was over, she felt practically dizzy. He looked a little dazed himself.

He bumped his Stetson up higher. "More than that and we'll end up in a stall in the barn."

She gave a shaky laugh. "We'd have to find a sitter for Jordan first."

He looked at her as if he was wondering if that was a possibility.

But she gave a little shake of her head. "Just kidding," she teased.

But his heated glance told her he knew she hadn't been kidding. He knew this passion between them was going to explode eventually.

She just hoped they didn't all get hurt in its shock waves.

After Marissa put Jordan to bed that night, she found Eli in the living room watching a Western series on one of the cable channels.

He looked up at her from the recliner. "Ty's in the barn with the new horses if you're looking for him."

"He's been down there awhile," she said.

"He's settling them in, making them feel at home. I'll listen to that monitor thing if you want to go talk to him." Eli nodded to the baby monitor on the end table. They could move it around to whatever room they were in and see Jordan in his crib.

"You sure you don't mind?"

"I don't mind. I'll just give you a call on that fancy phone of yours if I hear him."

She smiled at Eli. "Thank you. I won't be long."

She grabbed a jacket from the clothes tree in the kitchen before going outside. The November night air was cool, and she couldn't believe Christmas was as close as it was. She thought about everything Ty had told her today and understood better why he put so much store in her and Jordan being here for the holidays. She imagined the boy he'd been, missing both of his parents, trying to make the best of a life he didn't understand.

The scent of pine filled the night air as she walked toward the barn, her path well lit by a large floodlight. She zippered her jacket against the evening breeze. Her hair flew along her cheek as she gazed up at the thousand brilliant stars in the inky dark sky. There was only a sliver of moon peeking from behind a tall blue spruce.

She went in the side door. It creaked as it opened.

Immediately she heard the low rumble of Ty's voice. His tone was soothing and low as he spoke to one of the horses. The pregnant gray mare was a beauty with a white star on her forehead. Her mane and tail were darker than the rest of her coat. Ty was grooming her, running his hand over her flank before he used the brush. The sight of his fingers captivated Marissa. She knew those hands were callused and rough, but their touch was so sensual, taunting and gentle at times, utterly desire-filled at others.

She didn't think he knew she was there, until he asked, "Jordan all tuckered out?"

"He sure was. All that stimulation, riding in the truck, eating French fries. What more could a fourteen-month-old ask for?"

"Isn't that a good question?" Ty asked, as if he'd done a lot of thinking about it.

"He's bonding with you," she noted, watching Ty's expression.

"You mean he's starting to count on me."

"Yes. He smiles when he sees your face. He misses you when you're not in the room."

"It doesn't take much to make kids happy, does it?"

"It shouldn't," she offered. Then she said, "Thanks for telling me what you did today, about how you came to be with Eli."

"I just wanted you to know how I felt about responsibility and Jordan."

He put the grooming brush on the top rung of the stall and gave the horse a pat. Then he exited the enclosure.

"This mare—her name is Gray Lady—will be great with kids. I can tell. If we get any kids as guests, imagine that sparkle in their eyes as they watch us handle her foal."

"This is a whole side of you I've never seen," Marissa said. "Granted, I didn't know you well in high school. I just saw the wrestling star who had a crowd of friends. But at the wedding, I simply saw the charming cowboy who swept me away for a night."

"Don't start glamorizing me, Marissa. I'm just doing the best I can with what I've got."

"You have a lot."

"You mean the Cozy C?"

She didn't know what impulse came over her, but she reached up and touched the lines along his eyes. "You have character, Ty."

"Unc would say I *am* a character."

"He'd be right," she agreed with a small laugh that quickly died as his arms went around her.

"Marissa," he whispered right before he kissed her.

Her name had never sounded so beautiful. She knew

she shouldn't give in to the excitement or anticipation. And she wouldn't think about what could happen next. She was totally engrossed in Ty's scent, the feel of his beard stubble as she caressed his face. She wanted to touch him in ways no woman ever had.

His mouth was greedy. There was a wildness to the kiss that hadn't been there in the others. He slid his hands into her hair. His fingertips gently tugged on her curls. When she moved her hands from his face and wrapped her arms around him, they were as tight together as two people could be.

Feeling his arousal, she knew she was just as aroused as he was. She hadn't unleashed these feelings since the night Jordan was conceived. She'd forgotten how good desire could feel. Since the day she'd spotted Ty at the physical therapy center, they'd both been keeping a lid on their attraction, but now it burst free. Her heart thudded so hard it was the only sound she could hear. Their passion flared hotter and hotter as their tongues stroked against each other.

Ty broke the kiss. "There's an empty stall and a blanket to cover the hay with."

As she gazed into his eyes, she saw what he wanted. It was exactly what her body was telling her she wanted, as well. But all the wanting in the world couldn't douse the fear that making love with Ty could be an even bigger mistake now than it was the first time.

"Not a good idea," she responded softly, her throat tight, making it hard to get the words out.

Instead of asking why, he said, "One of these days you're going to forget you're Jordan's mom and remember you're a woman with desires that need to be filled."

"Never at Jordan's expense," she protested.

"I didn't say it would be. But denying the chemistry between us isn't an answer, either."

"I'm not denying it. I'm just not giving in to it."

She backed away from him and realized she could be putting a wedge between them. Was that what she wanted? So she didn't have to get too close? So she didn't have to put her trust in him? So she didn't have to make any decisions about a relationship with him?

"Eli's listening for Jordan. I'd better get back to the house." It wasn't a great excuse, but it would have to do.

Ty saw it for what it was. "And one of these days, you're not going to use Jordan as an excuse. One of these days, you're going to stop running from me."

Ty's prediction could be true. But tonight she was going to hold on to her heart and her sanity. She was going to take the safe route and do the right thing.

However, after she left the barn, after she left Ty, doubts plagued her and she knew sleep wasn't going to come easy tonight.

Chapter Eight

Taking care of a baby wasn't as easy as Marissa made it look, Ty thought on Sunday, knowing he had something to prove today.

He had been caring for Jordan since Marissa got home from church around eleven-thirty. After she'd changed, she'd set out for lunch at Raintree Winery with Jase and Sara and Amy. She'd told him Jordan had been a perfect little gentleman at the church service and she was hoping he was in one of his angelic moods today.

Angelic, Ty's eye.

As soon as Marissa was out the door, Jordan had started making his needs and wants known.

Sitting in his high chair now, Jordan banged his spoon on the tray, acting like a little tyrant.

"Need help warming up that food?" Eli asked, amusement in his tone that Ty didn't appreciate at all.

"Of course I don't need help. Marissa left instructions on how long to warm it."

Eli chuckled. "I had a late breakfast. You feed Jordan. I'll go clean some of that new tack you bought. Not too strenuous for an old codger like me."

"Unc, you can do anything you think you can handle around here."

"Clint's taken over most of my chores," he grumbled. "And that new hand will probably take the rest."

"I'm sure you can find something to keep you busy," Ty suggested, taking the dishes of baby food and applesauce to Jordan and setting them on the tray.

His little boy looked up at him and grinned. Ty almost forgot about the past hour when nothing he'd done with toys or walking around the house had seemed to please his son.

"He just misses his momma when she's gone," Eli offered.

"He's fine in The Mommy Club day care."

"Yeah, well, you're still a stranger to him. Give it time."

Ty studied his son as Jordan dipped his spoon into the applesauce and splashed it all over his shirt instead of putting it in his mouth.

Sucking in one of those long breaths he used when he was revving up for physical therapy, Ty pulled over a chair in front of Jordan and sat facing him, eye to eye, man to boy.

"If you think you can frustrate me until I go away, you're wrong. I'm here to stay, little guy. We're going to figure out what you like to do with me, how much horses are going to play a part in your life and most of all—" Ty picked up the baby spoon and wiggled it at

Jordan "—you're going to learn to eat a lot more neatly. That might be easier with finger food. We had scrambled eggs for breakfast, thanks to your mom. But how about pancakes for lunch? I make the best flapjacks. You can break them up and dip them in syrup and butter. What do you say?"

Jordan took his spoon, dipped it into the applesauce again and let it slosh onto the high chair tray.

"That's what I thought," Ty said, getting to his feet, knowing these were going to be quick pancakes.

The pancakes were a hit. Jordan even grinned at him as syrup dripped down his chin.

After cleaning up Jordan and the high chair tray, Ty enjoyed a quick pancake himself. Then he changed his son and slipped a clean shirt over his little boy's head. As Jordan gazed at him with those big brown eyes, Ty's heart melted and his fingers fumbled. He had a lot to live up to, and a lot to provide for this little boy. He bent and gave Jordan a kiss on the top of his head, feeling awkward, but also feeling like Jordan was his best accomplishment ever.

They went to the barn after that, and Jordan clutched at Ty's shirt collar, bobbed his head in all directions, maybe looking for adventure instead of his mommy. At least that's the way Ty saw it. This morning when they'd walked outside, maybe Jordan had expected to see Marissa. When he didn't, he'd got out of sorts. But now, he knew his daddy was taking care of him, and his dad would provide different entertainment than his mom did.

The afternoon passed more quickly than Ty imagined it would. Jordan felt hay in his chubby little hands, sat in a saddle in the tack room and ran around the barn chasing kittens.

"We'll be taking them to the vet soon," Ty told him. "Maybe you could bring one into the house and have it as a pet."

Somehow Ty could almost hear Marissa say Jordan was too young for a pet. She might like a kitten, though. She seemed like the type.

The type. He'd never thought someone like Marissa would exactly be *his* type. That night, after the wedding, she'd been wild and impulsive, and very different from the girl he'd known in high school. He knew now she wasn't always wild and impulsive. She was still that girl from high school, the one who was down-to-earth, smart, headed in the right direction.

Jordan was still giggling at a kitten's antics when Clint came into the barn.

Clint said, "The cabins are ready for any furniture you might want to put in them. The space heaters are running fine, and the plumbing's tip-top. You're going to be ready, Ty."

"We don't have any guests signed up yet. I'll concentrate on that this week."

Jordan reached for the brim of Ty's hat. Ty let the little boy tip it, and then he set it back on his head the right way.

"How did it go this afternoon?" Clint asked, studying the two of them.

"We had a rocky start. But we're doing better now. Babies are just like anybody else. They have to get used to you."

"Like you and Marissa getting used to being parents together?"

Ty thought about that kiss last night. He thought about his bedroom and what he really wanted. But what did Marissa want?

"We're settling in."

"I talked with John Vega and Troy Gunthrie last night. They're heading to a holiday rodeo in San Diego. Lots of events and a big purse."

"Like a carrot dangling in front of you, isn't it?" Ty said.

Clint gave him an odd look. "Is that what you were always doing, chasing the carrot?"

"Pretty much. I didn't have anything else on my mind, except maybe that I was going to show up my dad because I wasn't going to die rodeoing. That and the fact that the rodeo life represented freedom."

"I get that," Clint assured him. "But at what point does that life trap you, too? Getting older has made me wonder what's next."

"Sort of like a pro football player giving up his jersey?" Ty asked.

"Yeah, I guess it's like that."

Suddenly Ty heard someone clear her throat. When he looked over his shoulder, he saw Marissa. How long had she been standing there and what had she heard?

"Hey there," he said. "You're back. Did you have a good time?"

"Sara cooked a terrific meal. She has a bit more finesse than I do in the kitchen. Ethan was there, too, Jase's dad. He was telling us about his travels to wineries in Europe."

"Are you thinking of going there someday?" Clint asked.

"Italy sounded beautiful, but..."

She went over to Jordan and held out her arms. "I missed you, buddy. How was your day?"

To Ty's surprise, his son held on tight and didn't want to let go.

The look in Marissa's eyes was disappointment and maybe a little hurt.

"So you had a good time with your dad," Marissa said, working a light note into her voice. "That's great."

Clint tipped his hat and said, "I've got some work on the bunkhouse. I'll see you folks later."

Once Clint had exited the barn, Marissa tried to act casual. "How did it go?" she asked, still looking as if she wanted to take Jordan from his arms.

Ty went over to sit on a stack of hay bales and set his son on the ground. He figured it might be an easier transition for Jordan to go to his mom.

Marissa perched on the hay bale beside him and Jordan toddled over to her, clasping her knee. Ty could tell she wanted to pick him up and just hug him to death. But maybe she wanted to see if he'd stay with her or go back to Ty.

"It sounds as if Clint is really ready to settle down," she said.

"He seems to be." Ty paused a moment, and then added, "And you're wondering if I really am, too."

"Of course I am. Jordan is getting more and more attached to you."

"He's still always going to be attached to you," Ty said gently.

She met his gaze then. "I never thought he wouldn't want to come to me."

Ty dropped his arm around her shoulders, and just that casual gesture felt so right. Being near Marissa felt right. Yet part of him was fighting it, fighting what they could have together. Why was that? Maybe because he wondered if he was really the man she'd want in her life. Maybe because of their circumstances. He was Jordan's father, so he was a man she couldn't shove out of her life.

"I think a child as young as Jordan needs a mom more than a dad," he admitted.

When Marissa started to protest, he held up his hand. "I'm not saying I don't want to do the things you have to do—like changing him and feeding him and putting him to bed at night. I'm just saying he depends on you for those, and maybe he'll come to depend on me, too. But it's all going to take time. I'm somebody new who's showing him new things. But that doesn't mean he doesn't need or want you, too. We're in this together, Marissa."

He still saw the doubts in her eyes. "I know when your father left you felt a hole in your life."

"We weren't close," she murmured.

"I'm not sure that matters. When my dad left me with Uncle Eli, I felt that hole, too, even though I also felt he didn't want me around. Kids are meant to have parents, and when there's a glitch, they feel they're to blame if they're old enough to have sense about them. You and I were. And that doesn't make it easy for either of us to trust. But at some point we're going to have to. I hope this afternoon shows you you can trust me with Jordan."

Her son was looking up at her now and suddenly he raised his tiny arms to her.

Marissa folded hers around him and lifted him up onto her lap. She was smiling again. She was essential in her son's life again.

But she hadn't commented on what Ty had said, and he wondered if either of them could trust enough to make co-parenting work.

After Marissa put Jordan down for his nap, she found Eli rooting around in the refrigerator.

He glanced over his shoulder at her. "I'm looking for that last dish of apple cobbler you baked last night. Jordan didn't eat it, did he?"

She laughed, went to the refrigerator and pulled out a plastic container that was stowed away in the back.

"I put it in here to keep it fresh. Is this a snack or dessert before dinner?"

"It's a snack. It seems like we just keep eating up all that good stuff you make."

"How about vegetable soup and biscuits for dinner? And maybe, just maybe, I can bake some chocolate chip cookies."

"Yep, you sure do know how to cook," he said with a nod. "But you know, Ty hardly had any lunch. He was too busy with Jordan."

Ty could chow down with the best of them, and Marissa was surprised by that.

"Then I guess I'd better make sure I have plenty of soup, biscuits and chocolate chip cookies."

Eli took the container, went to the drawer for a fork, then sat at the table. He popped the lid open. "So chances are good you're going to stay for Christmas?"

When Marissa didn't answer right away, Eli went on, "A young boy should have both parents around for such an important holiday."

"I'll stay if Ty wants me to."

She pulled a soup pot from the lower cupboard and set it on the stove.

"If I want you to what?" Ty asked as he came in the kitchen door.

"You want her to stay for Christmas, don't you, boy?" Eli asked him.

"Sure," Ty answered offhandedly, and Marissa couldn't tell how much her staying would mean to him.

"That's settled, then," Eli said with a grin. Three bites later he finished off the cobbler, then he pushed his chair back. "I'm going to take a little rest myself. But listen, you two, if we're going to have a child around here for Christmas, we'd better start getting ready, don't you think?"

Eli left the kitchen, went into his bedroom and shut the door.

Ty crossed to the sink to wash up. After he did, he waited until Marissa had rummaged in the refrigerator for carrots, celery and an onion before he said, "Would you like me to light a fire? It's starting to drizzle out there, and it's pretty damp."

As soon as Marissa's gaze found Ty's, she knew they didn't need a fire in the fireplace to get a blaze going between them. The cozy idea of it appealed to her, though.

"We'll have to teach Jordan to stay away from it."

"We will," Ty said with assurance, his eyes locked to hers.

"I've always dreamed of sitting by a fire on a damp night."

"Then you've come to the right place."

There was that tempting note in Ty's tone that said an invitation to his bedroom wasn't faraway.

"I hear you didn't have much lunch."

"You know, I think the old man has eyes in back of his head, and ears in his toes."

Marissa laughed. "Like every real parent should. Essentially he was your dad, Ty. He's looking out for you."

Ty leaned against the counter and crossed one long leg over the other. "I suppose he is. That's why he wants to get Christmas all lined up. Do you really want to stay?"

"Do you really want me here?"

She knew those questions went back to their conversation in the barn, and both of them had to be honest.

"I want you here," he said.

"I want to stay," she said at the same time.

He came closer to her then and took the carrot from her hand, setting it on the counter.

"What do you have in mind for Christmas?" he asked.

"A tree for sure and a wreath on the front door. I'm sure Jordan would like some bells here and there. I'll have to think about the rest."

She was finding it hard to breathe, let alone think with Ty so near.

"After you're done thinking, make a list. The next time I go to town, I'll pick up whatever you need."

"I can find plenty of evergreens right here to make wreaths."

"You know how to do that?"

"With the internet at my fingertips, I can do anything."

He chuckled, his large hand coming up to cup her cheek. "I'm beginning to believe you can."

Her breathlessness had become so serious she was

dizzy. She took a step away so she wouldn't start trembling all over at the idea of being held in his arms again.

"Do you think you'll be ready for guests after the new year?" she asked.

A disappointed look passed over his face, and she was almost surprised he let her see it. He was good and shuttered when he wanted to be.

He ran his hand through his hair. "The cabins are finished. We just have to furnish them."

"The secondhand store's open tomorrow evening. I can go look around, or we can both go."

"We can both go. I'll take the truck because I'm sure we'll find something."

"You know," she said thoughtfully. "We can plan an open house for New Year's Day. It's not too late for that. We have a few weeks."

"An open house," he mused aloud. "You mean so folks can come and see the cabins and see what we have to offer?"

"Exactly. I can send press releases to radio and TV stations, and newspapers. We can plan a social media event, too, for that week in between Christmas and New Year's Day. We can have a Cozy C launch party. I've planned those kinds of things for the winery."

"The website will be ready by next week," Ty said. "Maybe the designer can create banners and ads, and we can send the files to local businesses so they could put links on their websites."

"Not just local." Marissa made a sweeping gesture with her hand. "Social media can be worldwide. If Jase says it's okay, we can advertise the Cozy C on Raintree's website, too."

"I'll talk to him about that tomorrow when I see

him," Ty acknowledged. "The thing is, Marissa," he said with a frown, "I don't want to overburden you. You've got a full-time job and Jordan."

"And time in the evening after Jordan goes to bed. I'm strong, and I don't need much sleep," she added.

This time he backed her into the corner where cupboard met cupboard. She wasn't going to take a step back or escape him.

"I like strong women," he told her. "Strong ideas, strong opinions, strong passion."

He was saying he knew her passion was strong, that her desire could meet his. They'd proven that before. Since their night together, their kisses had taken them near the passion they'd once shared. She could see he wanted one of those kisses now. Didn't she?

Ty smelled like the outdoors and the hay in the barn and so very male. His blue eyes caught her and held her and she couldn't look away.

"Eli's right through that door," she said shakily.

"Once his head touches the pillow he starts snoring, and he doesn't hear a thing. Not that there will be anything to hear," he said. "We'll be too busy kissing. Unless, of course, you let me take you on the table."

Laughter bubbled up from inside of her. Ty was so outrageous sometimes. Outrageously sexy. She was still smiling when his lips came down on hers.

Ty's kiss wasn't as seductive as it was fervor-filled. She realized they'd gone beyond coaxing. They'd gone beyond temptation. They both knew that this was exactly what they wanted—and more.

At that moment, maybe she finally accepted the fact that Ty was Jordan's father and would be staying in his life. He would be in *her* life, too. Could she convince him that a life here in Fawn Grove could be as rich and fulfilling, if not as exciting, as a life on the road, visiting new places, seeing new people?

As Ty's tongue traced her lips, she shook from wanting him, from the erotic pleasure he could give her. She thought about the table and what he'd said, and how exciting that would be. Reaching around him, she grabbed hold of his denim shirt and wished he wasn't wearing it.

Sensual pleasure caught fire in every nerve in her body. His hands were in her hair now, and each sweep of his tongue, each touch of his fingers stoked her desire as well as his. His hands left her hair, went to her back waist and slid under her sweater. His fingers were long and callused and deliciously enticing. A moan escaped her lips as his hands passed up her sides and came around to her breasts. He put a little space between them and pushed her sweater up. When his hands cupped her, she moaned into his mouth. After she pulled his shirt from the back of his jeans, she slid her fingers along his waistband. and this time, he groaned.

"You are so intoxicating," he murmured into her neck. "Like fine whiskey I'd never tasted. But when I finally did, I couldn't get enough of it. That table isn't so faraway," he said, making her aware with his body of what he wanted to do.

She almost gave in. She really almost did. But what had she told Jase? She didn't make impulsive decisions anymore. The consequences were too great, the responsibility too grave. When she made love with Ty again, she had to know in the deepest recesses of her heart that it was the right decision to make.

Although she didn't want to, although she didn't know what his reaction was going to be, she pulled away. He held on tightly for a few moments, but then he released her.

She still didn't have the answer to an important question, and it was time she did before they got more serious, before she gave in to a need that could blow up her life. She needed to know something. This probably wasn't the best time, but they were alone, and she wanted a few answers.

Swallowing hard, finding her voice, she said, "Tell me about Darla."

Instead of the eye roll or the rigid set of his jaw that she expected, he sighed. "You're determined to break the mood, aren't you?" he asked.

"My question is part of the whole mood. You can't expect me to just fall into your arms when I don't know who was there last."

He eyed her steadily to see how serious she was. Then he motioned to the table and chairs. "All right. We'll have a discussion at that table instead of using it for something else."

She felt herself blush, and she wasn't sure even why, except maybe she wanted the experience of making love with him on that table, too.

The coffeepot was always on. Eli and Ty often both stopped in for a cup throughout the day. Now Ty went over to it, took two mugs from the mug tree and poured them both a cup.

Maybe he was stalling a bit, but he went to the refrigerator and poured milk in hers. When he brought it to her, she added a teaspoon of sugar from the bowl on the table.

They sat next to each other and his thigh brushed hers. He took a sip of the coffee and eyed her over the brim. "For some reason, your coffee's better than what Eli and I ever made."

She didn't respond. She just waited. For whatever reason, this was hard for him. She'd give him leeway, and she'd be patient.

He must have seen that because he took another sip and set down his mug and leaned against the chair back. That movement increased the space between them.

"I met Darla in Texas," he began. "She was one of those red-boots-straw-hat women who barrel raced. We saw each other at a couple of rodeos and went out for drinks."

"And then one night…" Marissa prompted, unable to keep quiet any longer.

"It wasn't exactly like that," Ty protested. "Yes, we were attracted to each other. But we had rodeoing in common, too. We knew a lot of the same folks. She understood the circuit."

Marissa had thought maybe theirs had been a one-night stand. *Like your own one-night stand?* the little devil on her shoulder asked. But she ignored that for now. Whatever Ty had had with Darla sounded more serious, as if they could have made a life together. She was dying to ask what happened but she knew she had to be patient.

After a few more swallows of coffee, Ty turned the mug around within his large hands. "I thought I was a good judge of people," he said. "Of women. But I had Darla pegged all wrong."

"What do you mean?"

"It took me a while to figure it out, but she liked the idea of dating a prize-winning rodeo cowboy. After my accident and prognosis, I found out she wasn't keen about hanging with a cowboy who was no longer able to compete."

"She broke up with you after the accident?"

"Oh, yeah. She dumped me not long after I had surgery. She was honest about it. I have to give her credit for that. I mean it was clear I was never going to ride bulls again. The truth was I didn't know if I'd be able to ride period. She even talked to my doctor to get the bottom line."

"You were that close? Close enough, I mean, that the doctor would talk to her?"

"That close," Ty said. "I'd even looked at engagement rings."

It was easy to see now why Ty had his own trust issues, besides the fact that she hadn't told him about Jordan. After all, his mother had left. His girlfriend had done the same when the going got tough.

They really were quite a pair.

As much as Ty's trust issues, she was worried about something else. "That wasn't so long ago," she noted. "How do you feel about Darla now?"

"I don't feel anything," he admitted.

"Maybe you just numbed yourself."

He shook his head vehemently. "Not at the beginning—because it was easier to be angry about our breakup and hurt about her desertion than it was about my recovery and rehabilitation. I went through all of that. But when I came back here to help Unc, when we started making over the Cozy C, I realized what was important. I realized I had been wrong about her and it was a good thing I got out while the getting was good. I don't have any regrets because hooking up with her could have been a lot worse. A marriage with her would have had divorce stamped on it before our signatures were dry."

"I'm sorry that happened to you."

He pushed his chair back and got to his feet. "It's over, Marissa. Done and finished. Now I'm a dad, and nothing's more important than that."

But Marissa knew after what had happened here a few minutes ago that they, she and Ty, could become as important—if only the two of them could put aside the past and learn to trust.

Chapter Nine

Marissa was in the middle of breakfast the next morning when her cell phone buzzed. Eli and Ty were forking in scrambled eggs while Jordan pushed his around with his fingers.

Ty arched a brow quizzically as she answered the phone. She just shrugged because she had no idea who'd be calling at this time of day unless Jase had an emergency.

Then she saw the caller ID on her screen—Scott Donaldson.

"Good morning, Mr. Donaldson."

At that, Ty frowned.

"Good morning, Miss Lopez. Has Jase Cramer cleared you to take on outside clients?"

Donaldson's voice was warm and friendly yet a bit businesslike, too.

"Yes, he has. Do you still want me to plan a party for you?"

"I do. For Saturday, December 12. You have almost two weeks. Can you do it?"

"Do you have a guest list?"

"Of course."

"How many do you expect?"

"Thirty to forty."

"I can do it. But we'll have to consult. I need to know if you want your house decorated for Christmas, what you think your guests would like to eat and whether I can contact them by email or written invitation."

"You've thought about this," he said.

"I have. I like to be prepared."

"How about if I stop over at the Cozy C tonight? That way we can iron it all out, and I can talk to Eli again."

"Are you still trying to convince him to sell?" she asked, wondering if the consultation was the true reason for his visit or if it was further contact with Eli.

"I might be, but that won't be first on my priority list. I want you to get started on the party," he assured her.

"I often contract with the flower shop right here in Fawn Grove for flowers and decorations, too. I can work up a proposal on my lunch hour and have it ready for you tonight."

"You *are* organized."

"I try to be."

"Beautiful, smart and a good business sense. What more could a man want?"

The compliment was nice, but she wasn't sure she liked it coming from Scott Donaldson. Still, maybe he meant nothing by it.

Ty studiously kept his attention on the breakfast in

front of him when she ended the call and returned to eating.

"So you're going to do it?"

She looked up at him. "I'm going to write up a proposal and see if he accepts it."

Ty glanced sideways at her. "He's a flirt and a charmer."

"He's a potential client, and if Jordan wants to go to college someday, I'd better start saving now."

Eli harrumphed.

Ty went back to eating, and Marissa wondered what kind of reception Scott Donaldson would get when he came in the door of the Cozy C tonight.

That evening, around seven, Eli sat in the living room watching TV while Ty was checking on the horses in the barn. Marissa had given Jordan a few harmless utensils to play with and he used them to push around his blocks as well as banging them on the floor every now and then. When she'd gotten home tonight, Eli had let her use the computer in the barn to print out a proposal. Now it sat on the counter just waiting for Scott Donaldson.

She heard the vehicle drive down the lane and the purr of an expensive engine. A few minutes later, she heard a car door shut, and then the knock came on the door. But before she could pick up Jordan and go into the living room to answer it, Ty stepped inside, Scott right behind him.

Scott Donaldson had a thousand-watt smile for her. Ty's face was stoic. He had let the guy in but surely hadn't wanted to.

Donaldson came in first and glanced down at Jordan. "I think he's grown since I saw him last."

"Where did you see him?" Ty wanted to know.

"I got a glimpse of him at church on Sunday," Scott responded. "He certainly was well behaved for his age."

Ty looked from her to Donaldson as if they'd had some kind of secret meeting. Well, if he had questions, he'd just have to ask them later. She had seen Scott at church and waved at him, but that was about it.

Ty went to Jordan and picked him up from the floor. He said, "How about if we change you into your night gear? That will give your mommy time to *consult*."

"Thank you," she said, meaning it. It was hard to conduct a business meeting with a fourteen-month-old demanding her attention. It was plain to see that Ty understood that.

After he'd left the kitchen, she brought the proposal to the table. "Would you like a cup of coffee?"

"Sure would. I stop in at that expensive coffee shop in town every day, and I can't say it's worth it."

"No flavored coffee here," she joked. "Ty and Eli are straight caffeine cowboys."

She poured herself a mug and him one, too, careful not to get any drips on the table.

"How's business for the new year?" Donaldson asked.

"We just started the media campaign."

"So you're involved in that, too, Miss Lopez? Do you mind if I call you Marissa? I like to be on a first name basis with business associates."

That made sense, she supposed. "No, I don't mind."

"Then call me Scott. Okay with you?"

"That's fine," she said, sitting down across from him.

Instead of staying where he was, he moved his chair closer to hers, ostensibly to be able to read the proposal more easily. She could smell his cologne, something musky that smelled expensive. His suit was expensive, too, a navy wool with pinstripes. She guessed his tie was silk. When he first walked in, she'd noticed his cordovan loafers, a little different from Ty's boots.

He checked the first page of the proposal, her hourly rate, and seemed satisfied with it. Then he began studying the next page where she'd detailed the expenses—the flowers, decorations, food and servers. She'd spent a good portion of her lunch hour on the phone with the florist and the caterer.

Scott leaned back in his chair and gave her a grin. "I should have done this long before now. You've covered everything and I didn't have to spend a minute of time on it."

She laughed. "I hope I covered everything. Are you sure the hors d'oeuvres meet your approval? Anything on there can be changed. If you don't want the crab balls, we can go with stuffed mushrooms instead. The stromboli squares are always a big hit. We served them at the bachelor auction."

"I can see you've added a wine selection," he said. "Raintree Wines?" He arched an eyebrow.

"I based the prices on Raintree Wines, but if you'd like another brand, that's fine."

Now he laughed. "I'm teasing. Of course we'll use Raintree Wines. Only one thing I'd like to add. How about an open bar? Can you find me a bartender? Some of my contacts are strict bourbon drinkers, and they know good bourbon. How about Pappy Van Winkle's, fifteen year?"

She computed in her head and added a number onto the list of other expenses. "That's how much we'd add on."

"Marissa, I find this all quite affordable. I'm not sure

you're charging a high enough hourly rate. Just today you had to have spent at least an hour or two on this."

"Since you're my first client, the consultation and preliminary work were free."

He narrowed his eyes. "I'm not sure if that's good business, a way to make sure I hire you again, or if you're cheating yourself."

He was friendly and winsome and she liked his honesty. "Believe me, I'm not cheating myself. I can buy a bunch of diapers with this commission."

Again he laughed. Then he grew more serious. "So tell me something, Marissa. I've heard rumors about you and Ty Conroy. Are you living here permanently, or is this a temporary situation?"

Should she tell him it was none of his business? Why was he even asking? Then she thought about the hefty commission, and having him hire her for more party planning in the future, maybe even spreading the word about her services.

"This is temporary. Ty and I are just trying to find our footing as parents."

"I see," he said, leaning a little closer to pick up the pen.

Just then, Ty came into the kitchen, holding Jordan. Again he wore an expression that gave nothing away. Jordan was all changed, in his red, yellow and blue color-blocked pajamas.

"Time for Jordan's snack," Ty said, pulling the baby's high chair over to the table.

Scott said, "I guess I'd better sign on the dotted line." He did so, and then turned to Marissa. "If you have any questions, or any problems crop up, just give me a call. My cell phone's always turned on."

"I'll do that. The florist will probably want to set up in the afternoon on the day of the party. The caterer will set up about an hour before. Is that all right?"

"No problem with either. I'll make myself scarce so I'm not in the way. You'll be there to direct everything?"

"Of course." She could ask Kaitlyn or Sara to babysit now that this was a done deal. They often exchanged babysitting favors.

Scott extended his hand, wanting to shake hers. She let his fingers engulf hers and he held on a couple of moments too long, she thought.

But then he said, "It's good to do business with you. Can you email me a copy of the proposal?" he asked.

"Sure thing."

"Good night, then. I'll talk to you soon." His words had a husky, promising quality that made Ty's eyes narrow. When she would have accompanied him to the door, Scott said, "I'll touch base with Eli later. I can let myself out."

A few moments later, they heard the front door close.

Ty pulled a container of the cookies she'd baked from the counter, took out one and laid it on the tray of the high chair. "You two seem to get along well."

"Ty, this is business."

"And Donaldson knows how to do business. I heard him laughing. I heard you laughing."

"We were discussing his party and the kind of bourbon he wanted to serve."

Ty's brows arched. "Bourbon. He was sitting a little close to be discussing bourbon."

"Say what's on your mind, Ty."

"All right. He's got money, he's got looks and he's got flash."

"And what of it?" she asked. "I imagine if I have other clients who can afford a party planner, they're going to have all of those, too. By the way," she said, wanting to change the subject, "do you mind if I use your computer again to send him the proposal?"

"You're going to need a computer of your own, especially if you do more business like this."

"I can't afford one right now."

"You're welcome to use my laptop. It's usually on the dresser in my bedroom. It's more up-to-date than the one in the barn that we use mainly for record keeping."

It was in his bedroom.

She thought about standing in there with him. She thought about possibly lying in his arms in there. Scott Donaldson might have all the qualities that Ty had just mentioned, but he wasn't Ty Conroy. Her feelings for Ty were growing deeper, but she wasn't sure she should let herself fall for him all over again.

"I left my flash drive down at the barn," she explained. "I'll just use that computer for now. But I'll wait until after I put Jordan to bed."

"You don't need to wait," he said. "I know you want to take care of business. I'll give Jordan his milk and another cookie if he wants it. Go take care of business."

"Thank you," she said, meaning it. "Not for just giving Jordan his snack, but for taking him upstairs earlier. If I do start planning events outside of Raintree Winery, I want my dealings to be professional. I could do that tonight because of your help."

"Marissa, I want you to succeed as much as I want the Cozy C to succeed. Remember that, okay?"

She would.

The signed proposal was still in her hand, and she

couldn't help but be excited by the opportunity. With luck Scott Donaldson would throw more business her way. She was starting on her brand-new future—with or without Ty. Yet tonight, when Scott had asked her the question whether her staying at the Cozy C was temporary or permanent, in the bottom of her heart, she wished her stay was permanent.

Late the following Saturday morning, Marissa had joined in a conversation between Hannah and Eli in the living room. Hannah had brought a cake she'd baked from a new recipe as well as another casserole.

Jordan tugged on Hannah's arm. Hannah smiled at him and scooped him up onto her lap.

"Do you want in on this conversation?" she asked, tickling his tummy.

He giggled.

Suddenly the kitchen door opened and Ty came in. He looked like a man on a mission.

After greeting Hannah, he turned to Marissa. "How would you like to come with me to cut down a Christmas tree? We'll take the buckboard."

"So we're going pretty far?" she asked.

"Far enough to find a good one. I wouldn't want to bring one back and have you say it's too small, or it has a bare spot on the side."

"I'm not that particular," she protested.

His brows lifted. "I have a feeling you're going to want this one to be perfect."

Eli chuckled, too. "He's right, Marissa. You know he is."

"I'm not doing anything particular this morning. I

can stay and babysit," Hannah offered. She nuzzled the baby. "Jordan and I get along just fine."

Instinctually, Marissa trusted Hannah and her kind, nurturing way. "Thanks. I'll change him and give him a snack before I go."

But Hannah was already shaking her head. "Nonsense. You don't think I remember how to change a baby? Then we'll have fun with our snack. Eli and I can have another cup of coffee."

"I'll get my jacket."

Minutes later as she zipped her jacket over her pink blouse, she watched Ty harness Bruno, one of the larger horses, to the buckboard. His hands worked expertly, so strong and capable. But as she watched them, she imagined them on her skin. Whenever he touched her, he did it with such sensual gentleness. Whenever he kissed her, her universe rocked. Falling in love with Ty again seemed so natural that she didn't know if she could stop it. She had fallen in love with him that night they'd made love, yet she'd known it was a love that had no future. Now she was afraid to believe it could.

Ty laid a tarp in the buckboard bed, then climbed up on to the seat and patted the bench next to him. She climbed up too and sat, leaving about six inches of space between them. He jiggled the reins and clucked to the horse. Bruno started walking.

"Unc and I got our invitations to Donaldson's party. They were a surprise, especially mine."

"You both were on his list."

"Does he think some party is going to convince Unc to sell the Cozy C?"

From what she'd seen of Scott Donaldson, he was just covering the bases. "I think this party is about his business associates and contacts he's made. Whether or not you and Eli sell, you're contacts."

Ty was silent as he drove the buckboard over a rutted path just wide enough for it. It was bumpy but he didn't seem to notice. He seemed lost in thought.

Finally she said, "I feel like a pioneer crossing the plains."

"They weren't going in search of a Christmas tree."

"I don't know, Ty, they were searching for dreams. Aren't we doing the same thing?"

He made eye contact then, but didn't respond.

Suddenly he said, "Unc isn't talking to me about Donaldson's offer."

"Maybe he's not considering it."

"Selling the Cozy C would give him immediate security."

"Not necessarily long-term security, though," she suggested. "Whatever the amount is, it could seem like a lot, but Eli could live a long life. I just can't see him happy in a retirement home or living in a condo somewhere. Can you?"

"No, I can't. But this is going to be his decision to make. It's not a decision he's going to make now, but I imagine he'll think about it in the next year or two."

And just what would Ty do if Eli did sell? With rodeoing out of the picture, what would he want to do?

"The Cozy C website is getting hits," she told him, "and we're acquiring more social media followers now."

"Thanks to you. I think you brought everybody over from Raintree."

"I've checked the profiles of some of the followers. We even have some on the East Coast. We're getting there, Ty, really."

"I want to take more photographs of the Cozy C to post," he said. "That should create even more interest. The inside of the cabins, the horses in the pasture and the barns."

"People would be interested in the food you're going to serve, too. I could bake a few pies and take photos, get one of our beef stew and your uncle's chili."

"You do have good ideas."

"Just remember *that* when we can't agree on which tree to cut down," she teased.

Most of the time, Marissa forgot that Ty had had a knee replacement. Only when he came back from PT looking worn-out and heading for an ice pack did she wonder if he was in pain more than he was letting on. Today she thought he favored that leg a little as he got off the buckboard and carried the saw toward a grove of firs.

"I'm going to help," she said.

"Doing what?" he retorted.

"There has to be something."

"You pick out the tree and I'll cut it down. We'll be all set."

She knew that wasn't the bottom and top of it. She knew they'd have to drag the tree to the buckboard, and she could possibly help with that.

They dawdled around the trees, sizing them up. One grew against another and didn't have a back. Too many had big gaps in them that would be a problem for hanging ornaments. She was surprised at Ty's patience as she tried to decide.

The scent of fragrant pine surrounded them as they stepped between two rows of firs. Suddenly she saw it. The perfect tree.

"That one," she said with an excited note in her voice.

Ty looked toward where she pointed. They walked over to the seven-foot-tall tree and made a circle around it, studying it from every angle.

"I think you found a good one," Ty agreed. "Once we put it in the tree stand, it will almost reach the ceiling. It will be perfect in the stairway corner. We can mound Jordan's presents all around it."

"Do you have a tree stand?" she asked.

"I do. I got it last week. So we're all set. We can put it up when we get back."

She liked the idea of decorating the tree today and starting their holiday. "While you're sawing down the tree, I'd like to collect some pine boughs."

"I thought you might want to do that," he said with a smile. "I brought clippers. They're in the tin box in the buckboard bed."

Marissa fetched the clippers and began snipping pine boughs as Ty began sawing the fir close to the ground. She heard the tree fall.

"I can help you carry it to the buckboard," she called.

He called back, "No need."

She must have had her eyes on Ty, the breadth of his back, the straightness of his spine, the muscles in his arms that rippled under his long-sleeved T-shirt. She must have been admiring the slant of his jaw and noticing the tilt of his Stetson, because as she clipped an upper branch, she lost hold of it and it fell, scraping her cheek. She'd been intending to clip the softer boughs from it, but evidently distracted, she'd cut the branch, and now it bounced on her shoulder and fell to the ground.

She must have let out a little squeal because Ty immediately left the tree and came over to her.

"What happened?" he asked.

"Nothing major."

"You scraped your cheek," he said. "We should clean that off. I have bottles of water in the buckboard."

"Ty, really. I'm fine."

He took her hand and pulled her toward the buckboard, coaxing, "Come on."

Leaving her pile of boughs behind, she followed him, liking the feel of his hand enclosing hers.

At the buckboard he reached over the side to a six-pack of water. He tore one free and opened the top, then he pulled a folded red paisley handkerchief from his pocket.

"It's clean," he said with a smile.

"I don't need first aid," she protested again.

"We're just going to wash it until you get back to the ranch. Then you can put some antiseptic and salve on it. Your face is too pretty to have it marred by a scrape."

When she studied his face, she realized the compliment was sincere. "You really think I'm pretty?"

"I've always thought you were pretty. You were the prettiest girl in high school."

She scoffed at that. "Back then I didn't know what to do with my hair. It was just a fuzz of curls. I always thought my mouth was too wide and my nose was too short."

He put a finger over her lips. "Don't tell me those teenage insecurities still plague you."

"The night we hooked up..." she murmured, trailing off. Then she continued, "Why did you want to?"

"Why did *you* want to?" he tossed back at her as he gently wiped the scrape with the handkerchief.

"I thought you were funny and sexy and exciting."

He leaned away for a second. "Really?"

"Really."

"Seeing you all grown-up, more mature than you were in high school, I thought you were elegant, sexy and warm. When we talked, I felt good being around you."

"So it wasn't just attraction."

"Not then and not now. Besides, you're the mother of my son. That makes me look at our attraction in a new light. The closer we are, the better it is for Jordan."

She wasn't sure she believed that, but she could see Ty did.

He poured more water on the handkerchief and held it to the side of her face. Even with that cold water on her cheek, she felt her face growing warm. She was thinking about kissing Ty. She was thinking about doing more than kissing Ty.

As if he read her thoughts, he balled the handkerchief into his palm, leaned in and set his lips on hers. Every time they kissed, her knees grew weak. Every time they kissed she wanted more of him. Did he feel that way, too? She wanted to ask but she didn't want to stop kissing him.

He wrapped his arms around her, bringing her tight against him. Before she could guess his intent, he broke the kiss, swung her up into his arms and lifted her to the back of the buckboard onto the tarp he'd laid out for the tree.

He sat her on the edge and ran his hands through her

curls. "I want you, Marissa, and there's no one around for miles." Leaning into her neck and kissing her, he murmured, "I have protection in my pocket."

Ty was exciting...so exciting. Only he would think about making love here on the buckboard with pine trees all around them, and the sun shining down on them. He had protection, and she wanted him with an urgency that overtook her in a huge overwhelming wave.

She wrapped her arms around his neck. "Lay in the buckboard with me?" she asked.

His eyes sparked, the blue becoming deeper. "The wood's too hard. We can do it right here."

He meant to take her while standing right there, in front of the buckboard?

Before she could ask him, he unzipped her jacket and began kissing her all over again, and she lost her train of thought. As she dug her fingers into his hair, she flipped his Stetson forward. He laughed, swiped it off and tossed it into the buckboard.

"I don't need my hat and we'd better get rid of your jeans."

She knew her eyes were wide with anticipation and excitement as she became breathless at the thought of what they were going to do.

"No one's around for miles," she repeated, assuring herself of that fact.

"Just let go, Marissa. Forget about rules and standards and what you're supposed to do. Just go with it."

Kissing him, she *could* just go with it.

He unsnapped her blouse, unhooked her bra, and her breasts were bare to the warm sun and the breeze and the freedom that Ty seemed to embody. He traced her breasts with his fingers, and then brought his lips to her nipple. Teasing around it, he palmed her other breast, and she knew she was his no matter what he wanted to do.

She clasped his shirt, eager to feel his skin, too, and insinuated her hands underneath, sliding them up his chest, playing with his chest hair.

He groaned. "This isn't going to last very long with you doing that."

"It doesn't have to last very long to get us where we want to go."

He chuckled and she felt the rumble of it under her palm.

He unfastened her jeans and she unfastened his. When he pushed hers off, she could feel the cool tarp under her. He brought her closer to the edge of the buckboard. His jeans were unzipped but still hanging on his hips. He used his fingers in a most tempting way, arousing her, inflaming her, increasing her hunger for him until it was as great as his for her. When she didn't think she could withstand much more, he stopped, tore open a foil packet and prepared himself.

"Open for me," he said, and she did as he commanded. He gripped her backside, and then entered her swiftly, taking her breath away. She held on to him as he thrust harder and deeper. When she wrapped her legs around him, he kissed her so deeply she knew they had to be one.

Making love with Ty was like reaching up and finding a place among the stars. As he thrust into her again and again, she found pleasure like nothing she'd ever known. She called his name and with a groaning release, he murmured hers.

And as she held on to him, she knew she wasn't falling in love with Ty Conroy again, she'd already fallen. The question was—what was she going to do about that?

Chapter Ten

That evening, Marissa put supper dishes away while Ty set up the tree. Jordan played nearby in his saucer.

Eli called to her from the living room, "Can you come here, Marissa?"

She and Ty had avoided eye contact at supper—or maybe only she had. The pull toward him was so strong, she could hardly fight it. But she had to until she figured out what making love with him again had meant.

Had Eli noticed something different between them? He'd shot them curious glances but every time he had, she'd steered the conversation in another direction to keep him distracted from the electricity sizzling between her and Ty.

Maybe they were the only ones who could feel it.

"Be there in a minute," she called, folding the hand towel she was using and placing it on the counter. Scanning the kitchen, she saw there wasn't anything else that could delay her. And she knew if she didn't go into the living room, Eli would probably come get her.

When she scooped Jordan up and carried him into the living room, she was surprised by what she saw. Ty was threading lights all over the tree. She could tell they were those small twinkle lights that looked like tiny stars when they lit up. There were also two shopping bags overflowing with boxes containing shiny balls. She appreciated the holiday he was trying to create.

Could shiny balls and twinkle lights do it?

Only if what they were feeling for each other was as bright as those lights.

But Eli wasn't paying attention to the bags and new boxes or Ty threading lights on the tree. He motioned to a dingy old carton whose flaps were worn as he unfolded them.

"I know Ty bought that shiny new stuff, and you'll probably use it. But I wanted you to see these old ornaments. These are the ones I had when Ty was a boy."

Ty mumbled, "They're probably falling apart."

"You know that's nonsense," Eli said. "Things were made better back then than they are now. I bet you don't even remember most of them."

Jordan was wriggling by then to be let down. There was so much for him to get into.

"I got him these," Ty said, taking two trucks from one of the bags. He'd obviously extracted them from their boxes. One was a dump truck and the other was a four-by-four.

He set them on the floor and sat on the hassock beside them, running them across the braided rugs. "What do you think, Jordan?"

Ty had gotten his son's attention, and Jordan toddled over to the trucks and plopped down beside them.

Next Ty opened the box of plastic balls and dumped them into the truck. "There you go," he said. "Have a go at it."

Jordan clapped his little hands and looked up at Ty with the brightest smile.

Marissa's heart twisted. *Could* they be a family? Is that what Ty wanted? Or maybe he just wanted an affair without the strings of being tied down. He hadn't whispered words of love to her during or after they'd made love. He hadn't made any promises. He hadn't talked about commitment.

And what exactly did *she* want? A life here at the Cozy C? What kind of life would it be on a vacation ranch with strangers coming and going? What life could it be if she was afraid Ty would leave again?

Eli chose an ornament from the box. It was a small wooden train hanging from a piece of red yarn.

"This was one of the first ornaments I bought when Ty came to live with me," Eli said. "We were in the General Store in town. That was when we had a General Store. The owner made these to sell. When Ty saw it, he said he was going to take a train to faraway places, like all the places his dad had told him about."

"I was a kid. I didn't know much then," Ty objected.

"You knew enough to want to chase after your dad's dreams."

"Maybe so," Ty admitted.

Seeing that Jordan was occupied, he crossed over to the old carton and he lifted out another ornament. It was a cowboy on a horse, plastic and bright and eye-catching even all these years later.

He held it up. "Maybe I should have stuck to riding bucking broncos."

"Show me others," she said to Ty, wanting to know more about his childhood, the years he rarely talked about.

Ty shuffled through the box a bit until he found an ornament of a church that was white and sparkly. "This came in a set with other houses, a store and a stable. Unc got these the first Christmas after..." He paused. "After my dad left. He said the small town was just like this one. People went to church, hoping to find Christmas there. But it was really in that stable. I didn't know what he meant until he read me the Christmas story. Then I understood better."

"Can we find all of the village ornaments and hang them on the tree?" she asked, feeling that this would be important, not only for Ty and his uncle, but for Jordan, too.

"They should all be in there," Eli said. "Why don't you two look while I hang some of the other ones?"

Jordan was rolling the balls along the floor now, laughing as they ran into the sofa or the coffee table leg.

She and Ty sifted through the ornaments carefully. When her fingers brushed his, she felt fire and she pulled her hand away.

In a low voice he murmured, "You could come to my room tonight."

She kept her voice just as low. "Give me time to think about what happened and where we're headed."

He didn't argue with her. He simply remarked, "Time isn't going to change what happens when we touch."

She glanced over at Eli but he was busy hooking a frosted ball onto one of the high branches. She knew

Ty was right, but she couldn't just crawl into his bed as if they were a couple, as if she knew they were going to have a life together. Because she wasn't sure of that at all.

After they'd found the set of ornaments, Ty moved away from the box. "Go ahead and hang them on the tree. I'm going to go upstairs and get my camera. I want to take a picture of Jordan when we light it up."

Less than an hour later, as Jordan ate his bedtime snack, then rubbed his eyes with sleepy anticipation, all of the old ornaments and some of the new ones sparkled along the tree branches.

"We're ready," Ty announced.

Marissa picked up Jordan, holding him high and facing the tree.

"Watch the tree," Ty said to Jordan. "A big surprise is coming."

Then he plugged in the lights.

He'd bought a glowing star for on top, and Jordan's eyes were drawn to that first as it shimmered and blinked on the very tip of the tree. But then Jordan saw all the other lights twinkling, flickering on and off, and he giggled with glee holding his hands out, wanting to touch them.

"You can't touch," Marissa said. "It's just to look at. Isn't it so pretty? It's our very first Christmas tree."

Jordan chortled and leaned toward it. She took him closer. When he reached out to grab a little wooden sled, she said, "Look, don't touch," and she held on to his hand.

He might have made a fuss but Ty set down his camera and took him from Marissa's arms. "Come on, cowboy, I think it's time you got your pj's on."

Marissa watched Ty carry their son up the stairs.

Eli said, "I think he's going to be a right good dad."

In her heart, Marissa knew that Eli was right.

She was *sure* of this an hour later when there was a knock on her bedroom door. She opened it to Ty, who had a few papers in his hand.

"I wanted to show you these. I downloaded the photos from tonight and printed them out. I sent the pictures to an online processor and we'll get prints, too. But I thought you might want to see these."

Marissa had changed for bed. She hadn't grabbed a robe but her nightgown was cotton, not see-through. Still she felt a bit self-conscious because she saw Ty's gaze sweep from her neck to her knees, taking in the pink cotton, and maybe visualizing what was underneath it.

"You look good in pink," he said casually.

She felt herself blushing. The blouse she'd had on today had been pink, too. Like a video playing on YouTube, she could see Ty again, unsnapping the placket and slipping his hands underneath. He must have been envisioning the same thing. The heat between them was palpable. All she had to do was take a step back nearer to her bed and give him some kind of signal and he'd join her there in a second.

But seeing those photos in his hands, she knew that wasn't why he had come to her room.

When he handed her the printouts, she tried to forget about the pleasure he could give her. As soon as she saw the pictures, she did. She was holding Jordan. The expression on Jordan's face was pure awe and delight. And Ty had captured it.

"This is beautiful. His first look at his first Christmas tree. Last year when he was so small, there didn't seem to be a point to putting one up. And I guess I was still overwhelmed with taking care of him."

"You never told me what it was like." Ty's voice was husky and she could see he somehow wanted to capture those memories that she had accumulated.

"I didn't have a camera or a phone with a camera then. I had a month at home with him, but then I took him to day care. I hated doing that at first. I didn't want to be separated from him. But Jase gave me long lunches, so I could go to the day care facility and spend the time with him. The truth is, I was sleep deprived those first six months, so my memories aren't as clear as they should be."

"But then things got better?" Ty asked.

"Oh, yes. He started sleeping through the night, then I began feeding him solid food. When he was teething, I pulled some all-nighters, but for the most part, we fell into a good rhythm. I think babies like routine as much as adults do. After Kaitlyn and Sara and I became friends, motherhood became even easier. I had their support and they babysat now and then."

She looked down at the photos he'd taken, and then she said, "Ty, I'm sorry. I'm sorry you missed his first smile and his first steps. I'm sorry I didn't try to contact you."

"It wouldn't have been easy," he said, "with me moving around so much. But I did call in to check on Unc. I would have gotten the message eventually. I guess you really didn't know me, Marissa. Passing in the halls in high school, and one night in bed don't really tell you who a person is. Did you really think I'd never come back to Fawn Grove and find out?"

"I truly didn't know."

When she studied Ty now, she wondered if he'd ever be able to really forgive her for keeping Jordan from him. Would he ever be able to trust her? Did she trust him to be a father for day and night and forever?

She lifted the photographs. "Thank you for these."

"I did it for me as much as you. When the prints arrive, we can frame them."

As if their discussion had doused the fire he'd felt this afternoon, as if it had changed the air between them from electric to serious, he turned to leave. "I'll see you in the morning. Sleep well."

But as she closed the door, she knew she wouldn't sleep well. She knew regrets from the past were going to haunt her for a long time to come.

Ty came to the breakfast table after chores on Monday morning, looking distracted.

When Marissa set a plate in front of him with pancakes, hash browns, scrambled eggs and bacon and he didn't immediately pick up his fork, she knew something was wrong.

"What's the matter?" she asked him.

Eli, who had been tearing bits of pancake for Jordan, looked up at his nephew. "Something's wrong?"

Ty glanced at his uncle and made eye contact with Marissa. "Nothing's wrong…exactly."

She sat down beside him, knowing something was coming. She just wasn't sure what.

He took a piece of paper from his pocket that looked as if he'd carefully folded it into quarters. Now he unfolded it and laid it on the table. "When I checked my email this morning, I had received this letter in my in-box from a man in New York."

"New York?" Eli asked with a raised brow. "Is it somebody you know?"

"No, but he found our website. He did some checking. He knows I used to ride rodeo. He has his own software development business in Yonkers. He wants to bring four of his employees here and go on a pre-Christmas trail riding, camping trip. He saw that our official opening is January first. But these are his senior employees and he wants them to have this experience now. Something about they have a big project coming up in January and they'll be closeted together for long hours."

"Did you tell him no?" Eli asked.

"No. I'm thinking about it."

Eli looked as worried as Marissa felt.

"Are you physically ready for something like that?" Eli asked.

"I really thought I'd have longer to recuperate," Ty admitted. "I didn't think anybody would book until after the first of the year."

"So what are you going to do?" Marissa would be concerned if he did do it, concerned if he didn't. After all, this was what the new Cozy C was all about.

"He's a CEO," Ty said, almost to himself. "He could spread the word to other CEOs. It would be a new side to the vacation ranch business, bringing in teams of workers to refresh them. It's a whole other angle we could approach. If I do this, and do it well, we could pull in a lot more business."

"You could have Clint take out these tours," Eli suggested.

Marissa had been thinking the same thing, but Ty was already shaking his head. "No, I can't. *I'm* managing the Cozy C. *I'm* the one who came up with this enterprise. Sure, maybe Clint can help out later on, but I need him here handling the other work. I have to do this. I have to set the tone."

Marissa wanted to shout, *But what if you aren't ready?* Yet she couldn't voice that question, not here with Eli sitting there, too. Maybe later.

Maybe tonight.

Marissa thought about Ty and the trail riding trek all day. She took Jordan to day care and worked with Jase filling orders, collating invoices. Over her lunch hour, she finalized details for Donaldson's party on Saturday night by making a few calls, going over her lists, examining the menu again with the caterer. That afternoon, she worked on the after-Christmas winery tour event. Throughout it all, she tried not to let her mind wander to what could happen on a trail ride if Ty wasn't really ready for it.

Back at the ranch that night after supper, she made wreaths with pine boughs and red ribbon and attached jingling bells that made Jordan laugh. Eli helped her hang them on the barn door as well as the front door. Ty had gone out to do some work on the cabins.

Later, as she was saying good-night to Jordan, she heard Ty come up the stairs. He spotted her when she was exiting Jordan's room. With a quick glance at him, she saw that he looked tired. His square jaw held a day's worth of stubble. The shirt he'd changed into for supper showed signs that he'd worked hard during the evening, too.

When she approached him, he said, "I smell like horses."

"I don't find that altogether unpleasant," she teased.

He gave her an askance look. "My bet is you want to have a talk. I don't. My mind's made up. Mr. Brannigan and his team are flying in on Sunday. We leave on the trail ride on Monday, come back Wednesday, and they fly home Thursday. The deal's done."

"That's fast."

"It has to be with Christmas less than three weeks away."

"You've given this a lot of thought?" she asked, worried about him.

He must have heard her concern more than opposition because he didn't get defensive. "I've thought about it, turned it over and looked at it right side up and upside down. I want this, Marissa. I want to be part of it. Sure I could stay here and manage the ranch while Clint took out tourists, and maybe sometime that will be the way of it. But for now I have to run this program. Do you see that?"

She could see that. She just didn't want any harm to come to him. She moved in closer, wrapping her arms around his neck and surprising him. He looked wary, as if he thought she might try something underhanded. There was that trust issue again.

"Have you thought about talking to your physical therapist about this?" she asked.

"I called her this morning. She got back to me this afternoon. She thinks I should try it, being prepared for as many possibilities as I can. I assured her I'd take the portable mounting block, some pain pills I haven't used much up until now and I'll make sure I do my exercises while we're on the trail. I'll see her tomorrow for some last-minute pointers when I go in town for supplies."

"If you say you can do this, Ty, I believe you." She knew she had to support him.

"Your faith in me means a lot," he said in a husky voice.

Marissa could see strength in Ty—strength to start his life over, strength to try something new, strength to be the father Jordan always needed. His physique and his strength were two reasons she'd fallen for him the first time, reasons she ended up in his bed. But now, she was seeing so many different kinds of strength, not just physical but emotional, intellectual, entrepreneurial. His strength was the reason she had fallen in love with him all over again.

"If you can meet me in town over my lunch hour," she suggested, "we could go to that thrift store, maybe even the furniture store if we can make quick decisions. We have to remember to pick up dishes and pots and pans for the cupboards, towels for the bathrooms, a few decorations to make the cabins feel homey."

"So you have this all planned out. Do you have a budget?" he asked with a smile.

"I could show you what I came up with. Whatever it is, Ty, we'll stick to it."

"You run budgets for Jase?"

"When he introduces a new product, I run the prices on bottles, labeling and advertising. Then I use the budgets he provides. So I've gotten good at juggling."

Now Ty wrapped his arms around her and let his wrists dangle at her back waist. He brought her close, kissed her deeply, and then set her away.

"I want to ask you to my room, Marissa, but my

mind's going a mile a minute, and I don't want to be distracted when I'm with you. I've got a lot to figure out and not much time to do it in. I'm not too keen on going to Donaldson's on Saturday night, but I'm not going to leave Eli alone with him."

"I'll be there," she said.

"You'll be flitting from here to there taking care of the party. I don't want Donaldson getting Eli alone in his office and making some kind of side deal, not when things are about to take off here."

"It doesn't have to be a late night," Marissa said.

"No, it doesn't. At least not at the party. I'll probably be up late making sure everything is in tip-top shape and ready for guests."

She gave him a full-fledged hug. "It's all going to work out. You'll see."

She voiced the confidence she wanted to have, not the doubts she really had. If something went wrong on this trail ride, the whole new idea for the Cozy C could be over—and Scott Donaldson's offer to buy the Cozy C would be waiting.

Saturday evening, Ty looked around at the guests at Scott Donaldson's cocktail party. Most of the men wore suits and ties—*expensive* suits and ties. He wore a Western-cut suit he'd bought a few years back for special occasions. With a white oxford shirt and a bolo tie, it worked even for this shindig.

As he mingled, someone recognized Ty and asked about his plans for the Cozy C. The man had apparently visited the ranch's social media page.

That was the exact moment that across the room Donaldson took Eli aside.

Ty had to make a choice—drum up business or stand guard over Eli. He decided he had confidence in his uncle to stand up for himself. Still, he didn't like Donaldson's smile or the long talk he was having with Eli.

Ten minutes later, Ty broke away from his own conversation and spotted his uncle enjoying what Ty assumed was fine liquor at the living room bar where a bartender was on duty. Donaldson had spared no expense, and Marissa apparently had thought of everything.

After she'd left this afternoon to set up for this party, he'd cared for Jordan until Hannah had come over to babysit. Marissa had suggested they try Hannah to see if she worked out, and he'd thought the plan was a good one.

Thinking about Marissa, he scanned the living room for a glimpse of her, but didn't see her. Earlier at the party, she had waved once, and then disappeared. He wanted to find her. She was a sight tonight in a red cocktail dress that she said she'd used at Raintree Winery occasions. She looked fantastic, and put to shame all the women who had dolled up for this occasion.

Looking for her, he walked through Donaldson's house. It was large enough for two families to live in it, Ty thought, and perfectly appointed. A far cry from the homey feel of the cabins he'd just completed with Marissa's help. As he moseyed down a hall, he thought of the men flying in to the Cozy C tomorrow. He told himself he was prepared. He had everything planned out for their arrival and the camping trip. But even the best plans could go awry.

He knew he shouldn't think that way. Everything

was going to be fine, he told himself, for at least the thousandth time.

Hearing a man's and woman's laughter, he slowed as he neared a room near the downstairs bathroom. The door was partially open. He caught sight of a patch of red and he recognized Marissa's dress. He couldn't keep himself from peering in.

Marissa and Scott Donaldson were standing side by side, very close, examining something on a tablet Donaldson held in his hand. His other hand was on her shoulder. She didn't seem bothered by it at all. In fact, she laughed at something he said.

Ty studied the two of them—Donaldson in his expensive custom-made suit, the fabric luxurious-looking as it reflected the overhead light. Marissa was a class act with her hair upswept, her dress molding to her just right, her high-heeled shoes making her legs look curvy and oh, so tempting. At that moment, she and Donaldson seemed to fit together perfectly. Wouldn't any woman want a man like the developer? Accomplished, wealthy, successful. After all, Marissa had a son to think about. She had a future to plan.

Just what was Donaldson showing her on that tablet, and why did she look so darn interested?

Ty heard her say, "Thank you, Scott, that's a wonderful idea."

Donaldson responded, "This is my bailiwick. If I can be of any help to you, you know I will be. This is a great party you helped me throw tonight. You're fabulous at planning, down to the smallest detail."

Ty turned away from the doorway, having heard enough. Those two had a mutual admiration party going on in there. Plus, they seemed to have a familiarity he didn't like at all. As he made his way back to the party, he recognized the emotion that overtook him. Jealousy. The question was—what was he going to do about it?

Chapter Eleven

Later that night, once in the truck where they could finally speak in private, Ty asked his uncle, "What did Donaldson want?"

Eli glanced at him, then stared out the windshield into the black of night. "He upped his offer."

"To what?" Ty asked.

Eli named a figure that made Ty's head spin.

"Is it tempting you?"

Eli cut him a sideways glance and said simply, "It's an option."

An option. It was an alternative solution if the idea of a vacation ranch wasn't a success. The land was valuable. He felt that Unc believed everything was riding on the success of the trip of these guests arriving tomorrow. And maybe he did, too. It was a test run, but if he failed the test, what would that mean going forward?

When Ty and his uncle entered the house, Ty saw immediately from the monitor on the counter that Hannah had put Jordan to bed. She was sitting at the kitchen table having a cup of tea.

Her smile was practically adoring, and all for Eli, when she asked him, "Would you like coffee or hot chocolate? I can make some."

Eli seemed to consider the question for a long time as if it were very important. He glanced at the monitor to see Jordan was sleeping peacefully. "It looks like Jordan is settled in for the night. We can wind down with some hot chocolate until Marissa comes home."

Ty was surprised his uncle was finally consenting to spend some time with Hannah. Was Eli actually considering a relationship with Hannah after all these years of putting her off? And why? Because the Cozy C was worth so much money he felt like somebody now? If nothing else, Ty had to thank Donaldson for that.

Hannah was already on her feet moving toward the refrigerator for the milk. "I'll make real cocoa, not that stuff that comes in a packet. Marissa showed me where everything was if I wanted some."

Eli swiped off his hat and hung it on the rack. "Sounds good."

Hannah glanced over her shoulder as she pulled the milk from the refrigerator. "I brought oatmeal cookies, too, for Jordan. Are you interested?"

"I'm always interested in your cookies," Eli assured her.

That comment told Ty that his uncle was definitely mellowing toward Hannah, if not toward life. *Changes all around,* he thought.

Ty tried to leave the couple alone, but they insisted

he stay for hot cocoa. As they sat around the table, Eli and Hannah caught up with what was happening around Fawn Grove. Christmas celebrations in the square only concerned him as far as what he'd attend with his son— and Marissa. He'd never lived with a woman before. When he'd invited Marissa to come to the Cozy C with Jordan, he hadn't been sure how their lives would mesh. He thought they'd meshed just fine. But what did she think? Was she looking forward to spending the holidays with him, and planning to stay well beyond the new year?

The next hour passed quickly as he thought about spending his first Christmas with his son. But he couldn't stop thinking how sexy Marissa had looked tonight in that red dress. Lost in his reverie, he suddenly perked up when he heard a car outside on the gravel lane. It wasn't long before a car door slammed and Marissa came in the back door.

She grinned when she spotted Eli and Hannah sitting side by side, and her whole face lit up with that smile. "Are we having an after-party?" she asked.

Looking a bit flustered, Hannah stood. "Just cookies and catching up. Jordan was as good as gold tonight. He didn't even make a fuss when I changed him into pj's." She motioned toward the monitor. "I think you'll have a calm night."

"That I could use," Marissa responded, finally glancing toward Ty.

When their eyes met and held, he knew nothing was calm about the chemistry between them. Did she see that? Or did she see a future with someone like Scott Donaldson more clearly?

"I'd better be going," Hannah said.

Pushing his chair back, Eli stood, too. "I'll walk you to your car."

Though she blushed a little, Hannah didn't protest.

"Something new there?" Marissa asked with a quirked brow as the couple left the house and she set her purse on the counter and checked the monitor once more.

"I'm not sure. I think Eli has finally realized that on paper he's a rich man. Donaldson upped his offer for the Cozy C tonight. That offer seems to have given my uncle a little more stature and a lot more confidence in himself."

"Because he's considering selling?"

"I don't know," Ty said honestly. "I think he's holding his breath to see how this week goes. The success of it is on my shoulders."

Marissa didn't try to tell him it wasn't.

"We should get to bed," Marissa said. "You have an early day tomorrow."

Get to bed. Ty pictured exactly what had happened when they'd gone to cut down the Christmas tree. He could see in Marissa's eyes and from the expression on her face that she was remembering, too.

Afraid she'd back off, afraid their chemistry would scare her away again, he brought up a safe topic. "You pulled off a great party. Everyone looked as if they were having a good time. The food was terrific. I bet Donaldson will spread your name around."

"Thank you," she said, looking surprised at his words, but pleased. "It did go smoothly. If he does give my name out to his friends, and they want parties, I'll have to decide what I'm going to do. I don't want to leave Raintree, so I'd have to limit what I take on. I don't want to miss Jordan being a baby. I don't want to miss precious moments I can never recapture."

As soon as her words were out of her mouth, the air around them seemed to become charged. She'd taken away from Ty lots of those precious moments, and he could see on her face that she knew it.

"Ty—"

If she was going to apologize again, he didn't want to hear it. He understood she was sorry, but that didn't make up for the time he'd missed with his son, the moments he couldn't recapture. Did he want to go there tonight? No. Right now, he had other issues to discuss. Such as seeing her tête-à-tête with Donaldson. "You and Donaldson were in his office for a while. Discussing anything important?"

"Not really. He showed me some apartments he'd found that I might be interested in."

He felt as if someone had landed a solid punch to his gut. "You're seriously going to look?"

"I'm not sure what's going to happen next," she said.

"I don't get you. You were just going to apologize for keeping Jordan away from me for over a year. But now you're considering moving out. I've told you before I want to be his dad, day and night, all the time, not just on weekends, not just on the odd evening, not just after church on Sunday. I'm serious about that, Marissa."

Feeling as if he'd said too much, let his guard down too far, he muttered, "I'm going to go upstairs and get out of this monkey suit."

Before he said something he shouldn't, before he scooped Marissa up into his arms to carry her up to his bedroom, before he let their chemistry explode, he left the kitchen and mounted the stairs.

By the time he'd reached the second floor, Marissa had caught up to him. She clasped his arm, her fingers on him like fire even through the suit coat. That was the problem. He could feel her whenever she was close. In that instant, his body revved up as it had before a rodeo, and all he wanted to do was taste her and satisfy a primitive longing that he'd tried to satisfy with bull riding and winning big purses and seeing his name emblazoned in neon on the scoreboard.

But Marissa had nothing to do with scores and bull riding and seeing the sights in the next town he drove through. She was about the Cozy C and home and a sense of belonging he'd never really had. But he couldn't let her see he cared about that. He couldn't let her see just how important fatherhood had become to him. He couldn't let her see just how much he wanted her across the table from him every morning at breakfast.

Oh, no. He'd fought against vulnerability all his life. Now wasn't the time to let his guard slip too much, not when he had to have his head on straight about the importance of the guests coming in tomorrow. Not when Marissa was looking at apartments elsewhere.

Still she was holding on to him, looking at him with those big brown eyes that made him swallow hard and practically forget his name.

"You're never going to forgive me, are you?" she said. "That's why looking at apartments might be the right thing to do."

"It's not about forgiving, Marissa. It's more about forgetting what I've missed."

She looked so sad. She looked so lost in that moment that he followed his impulses instead of good sense. She'd been holding his arm, but now he pulled away in order to slide his fingers up her nape. He brought her face close to his and he looked straight into those deep brown eyes.

She blinked as if the intensity of the moment was just a little too much. That's when he kissed her.

The kiss turned hot and heavy right away. There wasn't any hesitancy on her part and definitely none on his. The momentum they'd experienced the day they'd cut the Christmas tree down seemed to build, and he swung her into his arms and carried her into his bedroom. He stood her by the side of the bed, then he turned on the bedside lamp and in a couple of strides shut the bedroom door.

"Jordan," she said.

"I'll leave it cracked," he responded, and opened it about an inch. Then he shrugged out of his suit coat, undid his bolo tie and asked in a low, husky voice, "Are you going to undress, or do you want me to do it?"

"I might need help with my zipper," she said softly.

"I'd be glad to oblige."

"I can unbutton your shirt," she told him.

"Are you telling me we're going to go slow this time?"

"I'm not sure what we're going to do," she admitted, and he knew she meant more than in this room, right now.

But in this room and right now was all he could think about. As he reached around her to find her zipper, she attacked his buttons. No, they weren't going to go slow. He could tell.

"Let's not think about tomorrow," he said. "Or next week or after Christmas."

She stopped for a moment as if she had to give his words consideration. "Deal," she said breathlessly.

* * *

Marissa hadn't made the deal with Ty lightly. She'd thought about climbing those steps to him before she'd done it. She'd thought about what she'd done to him and whether guilt had brought her to his bedroom. But it wasn't guilt. She wanted Ty, plain and simple. She wanted him in every way possible. She wanted to experience everything she could with him. Would he ever trust her enough to have a future with her? Could she forget he'd once been a traveling cowboy and believe that maybe that wanderlust wasn't still in his blood?

But according to the deal she'd made, she wasn't going to think about all that now. Those questions had done nothing but confuse her up until this point. Maybe analyzing life wasn't the same thing as living it. Maybe what she had to do was live it with Ty.

She couldn't see how dark the blue of his eyes was in the shadow of the lamplight, but she could feel the intensity of his gaze as he reached around her and pulled her zipper down its track. She pushed aside his shirt, laid her palms on his skin and sifted her fingers through his chest hair. She felt his groan rumble in his chest as he pushed her dress off her shoulders and it fell to the floor. She stepped out of her heels and reached for the band of her panty hose when he caught her hands and slipped his inside the waistband.

"I'll take care of these," he said in that voice that was so deep and sexy she could just melt in a puddle right then and there.

He did take care of the panty hose and all that was left was her bra and the black onyx beads around her neck. They'd been a gift from Kaitlyn last Christmas.

She'd worn a strapless bra tonight so she didn't have to worry about the cut of the neckline of her dress.

Ty's hands deftly went to the fastener of her bra at her back. He unclipped it. The bra fell away.

"I'm still amazed you're a mom," he said.

"I've gained a few pounds."

"Not that anybody would notice. You're so beautiful, Marissa. You take my breath away."

This was Ty. He could be charming, but he didn't use lines, and he said what he meant. Tonight she'd been uncomfortable with Scott Donaldson's remarks, when he'd stood too close, the way he placed his hand on her shoulder or on her elbow or at her waist.

She didn't want to move away from Ty. His words washed over her like sparkling fairy dust that could transform her into Cinderella. Didn't every woman want to be Cinderella? Didn't every woman want to find Prince Charming?

Ty didn't wait for her to help him remove his slacks and underwear. He shucked them off almost as quick as she could blink, then he motioned to the bed for her to get in. After he whipped back the spread and sheet, the wide expanse of the king-size mattress stared her in the face. This was his bed—where he slept, where he dreamed. Something powerful shook her in that moment, something that told her this was different than the other times they'd come together.

After she was on the other side of the bed, he chuckled. "Don't go too far. Light on or off?"

"On," she said. She had to see his expressions, to maybe get a glimpse of what he was thinking. She had to see his reactions to everything she did.

"After the daylight, this is kind of mellow," he remarked wryly.

"Even though it was daylight, we didn't see a thing. It was all so quick."

"But pleasurable," he reminded her.

"Maybe I want more than pleasure tonight," she said quietly.

For just a moment, he stilled. Did he understand that she loved him? That she wouldn't be here in his bed with him if she didn't? It was too soon to say the words. And even if it wasn't too soon, she was still afraid if she said them, he'd feel trapped. That's what she'd been afraid of all along if she told him about the pregnancy. She would trap him.

Ty shifted to the side and ran his hand down her shoulder. "I want to kiss you all over."

That was just a phrase, she told herself. He couldn't really mean all over.

But his lips started a journey. He visited her mouth for an exploratory but complete kiss that made her limbs tremble. When he trailed small kisses to her breast and flicked his tongue over her nipple, she clutched his shoulders with a ferocity he had to feel.

"Like that?" he asked with the Texas drawl he'd been born with.

"I like it all," she whispered. But she couldn't let him do it all. She couldn't let him give all the pleasure. She took his hand and she kissed his palm, letting her tongue flick out along his life line.

"Where did you learn that?" he asked with a growl. "My gosh, Marissa, you're setting everything on fire."

And that was her intention.

"If you think that's good," she warned, "just wait."

She kissed his chest, letting her lips trail down and down and down until she was at his navel.

"If you wanted to go slow, this isn't the way to do it," he growled.

"I don't care how we go as long as we get there."

"Marissa," he groaned, and pulled her on top of him.

She heard him pick up something on the nightstand and realized he must have put a condom packet there.

When he kissed her again, as if tonight were the only night left until the end of time, she let herself live with the kiss, live with the fire, live with the desire. Then she acted on it. She closed her hand around him and guided him into her.

He said gruffly, "I want our eyes wide-open this time. I want to see what I do to you, and I want you to see what you do to me. No masks, no quick kiss or goodbye afterward. This time we're going to deal with this, Marissa, the way we should."

She wasn't sure she wanted to do that. She was afraid to talk about the future. She might even be a little afraid of the future.

"Make love to me," she said to Ty, as she took him deeper. This was a taste of heaven—joining her body with his until they reached the sublime, or something even better—a union that was unbreakable, a union that could last.

Marissa accepted Ty's passion and returned it. She was his equal and she felt like it as he groaned and murmured her name. She watched his face as a dark flush crept over it, as his brows drew together and sweat beaded on his forehead. She wondered what emotions he was seeing on her face, and for a moment felt self-conscious. But then she didn't care. This was the two of them in the throes of raw desire, witnessing the truth in each other's eyes.

When his final thrust took her over the edge of desire into rippling pleasure, she knew her truth. She loved Ty Conroy, with all of her heart.

Afterward, as he lay his forehead against hers and they both closed their eyes, she wondered what his truth was, and if her Cinderella fairy tale had any possibility of coming true.

Excitement hummed all over the Cozy C the following day. It wasn't just generated by Marissa's night in bed with Ty. That had been heart-swimmingly wonderful, though doubts still plagued her. Did he want her to stay at the Cozy C only to keep Jordan close? Was she as important as his son? Were *they*?

Ty hadn't told her he loved her. He'd only shown her how hungry he was for her.

Even wonderful sex wasn't a substitute for love.

Ty had been distracted this morning, and she suspected his thoughts weren't about last night. He was concerned about the next few days and the trail ride and camping trip he might not be ready for. She was worried, too, but couldn't let it show.

Hannah had come over to help them get ready, although the cook Ty hired was going to take care of all the meals for the guests. She and Hannah decided to bake cookies and muffins for that something extra. The men could take the baked goods along, making meals around the campfire just a bit more inviting.

Hannah watched Jordan as Marissa took hot pans of baked cookies from the oven.

"He's going to be all right," she said in a motherly tone.

At first Marissa thought she was talking about Jordan, but then she realized Hannah was talking about Ty.

"I don't want to let him know how much I'm concerned."

"I know you don't. Eli's concerned, too. But Ty's been riding for more than a month. He knows his limits and what will happen if he pushes them."

"He hates using a mounting block."

"Eli says he has a portable one he can pull up onto the saddle after he's mounted. He has that special saddle, too, that's easier on his knee, and Goldie isn't difficult or in any way headstrong. Trust him, Marissa."

Could she trust Ty in oh, so many ways? Hannah seemed to be encouraging her to do just that.

When the huge SUV rolled in later that afternoon, Ty was there to greet it, looking like the ultimate cowboy in his Stetson, chambray shirt, jeans and boots. She and Hannah unabashedly peeked out the window.

After a few moments of conversation, however, Ty came to the door and motioned to her. She went to the screen door.

"Is Jordan still sleeping?" he asked.

"Yes, he is."

"I can watch him if he wakes up," Hannah offered.

"Great," Ty said. "Why don't you come along and show the men the guest cabins. Would you mind doing that? You're great at that kind of thing. I'll get Clint, and then give them a tour of the barn."

"I don't mind at all." And she didn't. If Ty was trying to make her feel part of the Cozy C, he was succeeding.

Hannah gave her an encouraging smile as Marissa snagged her jacket from the peg by the door and went outside to greet the men with Ty. There were five of them staying in two of the cabins, three in one, two in the other. They had declined to share the bunkhouse, which made Marissa and Ty both think that roughing it might not come easy to them.

Ty introduced her to Colin Brannigan. He had gray hair, black-rimmed glasses and seemed to be the oldest of the five men.

"Colin is CEO of Brannigan Incorporated. It's a software company specializing in gaming," Ty explained.

"You probably don't know much about that," Colin said with a laugh as he studied Marissa.

"You're right," Marissa acknowledged. "But I'm willing to listen…and learn. I'm sure as my son gets older it's something he's going to try to convince me he should be doing."

Colin gave a nod as if he liked her answer.

The other men—Mike, Sean, George and Brad— were all pleasant enough and insisted Marissa call them by their first names.

Ty told them, "Clint, my foreman, will see to your bags while I show you around."

"No cable in the cabins, I suppose," Brad remarked offhandedly.

"No cable," Ty agreed. "I told Colin that when he first emailed. But after the tour you can settle in, and then we'll have dinner in that small barn over there. Afterward we'll light a campfire, have some coffee and Marissa's brownies, then you can all tell me about where you're from and what you do. It will be good to turn in early tonight, since we'll be heading out after breakfast around 7:00 a.m."

"What time is breakfast?" Sean asked.

"Around six," Ty said. "Can you handle that?"

Sean laughed. "Heck, yes. I have to be on the commuter train by seven back East."

"Come on," Marissa said. "I'll show you to your cabins. The refrigerators are stocked and there's a coffeepot and snacks if you're hungry after your trip."

"No food on the plane," Mike grumbled. "Yes, we're hungry after the trip."

In addition to the sweets, she and Hannah had made up two trays with an assortment of cheeses and meats with crackers to accompany them. There were veggies, too, in case any of the men were watching their diet.

The men had questions as they walked to the cabins. How big was the Cozy C? How many horses did they have? Did they grow any crops?

She told them, "Since Ty took over management, things are changing. He's thinking about leasing some of the property to growers. He's added a few horses and one of them is pregnant. She's due to foal after New Year's."

"That's something my kids would like to see," Mike said. "Would you have anything for kids to do here?"

"We can supply board games and outdoor activities like horseshoes, croquet, badminton. But the real entertainment is in the hiking, spotting a deer or a jackrabbit, or following the trail to a watering hole for wild mustangs."

"There are some of them around here?" Brad asked.

"More up north," she responded. "But there's a herd that wanders around here, too."

The men seemed to mull this over as they went to the first cabin that she'd decorated in rusts, deep blues and reds—the colors of the Navaho blanket that hung on one wall. A fold-out sleeper sofa sat underneath it covered in deep blue denim. Most of the wood furniture they'd found at the thrift store, but it suited perfectly with its distressed nature and even antique bearing.

When Brad spotted the trays of cookies and cheeses and meats on the counter, he said, "This is nice."

Just the effect she and Ty had wanted.

After Colin, Mike and Brad settled in the first cabin, and Sean and George in the second, Ty appeared again.

"Do you think you'll be comfortable?" he asked them.

"Home away from home with better scenery," Mike said, and they all laughed.

Ty motioned toward the big barn. "My uncle's there ready to introduce you to the horses. I'll be there in a minute."

After the guests started walking that way, Ty pulled Marissa into the second cabin. "How did it go?"

"I think they were pleased, maybe even impressed."

"That's your doing," Ty complimented her. "You've put the *cozy* in Cozy C."

She knew that look in his eyes. She knew what he was thinking. They could have a tryst in one of these cabins, just for a change in venue.

He grinned at her. "I guess we can't try out the beds when we have guests ready to use them. But it's something to think about when they leave."

"You have a bed. I have a bed."

"You can never have too many beds or too many places to enjoy each other like we did last night."

Was he going to say it? Was he going to tell her what he felt?

But then he went on to say, "I'll be thinking about that the whole time I'm gone. If I had you in my bed tonight, I wouldn't get any sleep, and I need it for tomorrow."

She'd been thinking about what would happen tonight if he'd pull her into his room again. But she understood how he had to prepare mentally as well as physically for the next few days.

She slid her arms around his neck. "There's always the night after you get back."

When he kissed her, she thought she felt something more than passion in the kiss. But maybe she was deluding herself. Only time would tell.

Chapter Twelve

When Marissa returned home from work on Wednesday, she expected Ty to be there. She expected their vacation guests to be ready for a meal in the small barn near the bunkhouse, and then packing up their things to go home tomorrow.

However, when she came into the house with Jordan waving his arms in greeting to Eli, Eli's face looked a bit haggard.

"Is Ty back?" she asked, hoping Eli's answer would be, *Of course. He's down at the cabins with the guests.*

But that wasn't Eli's answer.

Ty's uncle answered tersely, "Nope."

"He hasn't called in?"

She knew cell phone coverage was spotty the farther Ty rode from the ranch. But on the return trip, the closer to home he traveled the better it should be.

"Do you think that boy's going to call and worry us with something?" Eli asked rhetorically.

"Like we aren't worried now," she said, setting Jordan on the floor so she could unzip his jacket, remove it and let him run toward his bin of toys.

Eli had no sooner stopped speaking than his cell phone buzzed from his pocket.

"I'm still not used to this dang thing," he said.

Eli didn't even check the number before he answered. "Ty, is that you?" A moment later, Eli glanced at Marissa and gave her a nod.

"Why aren't you back yet?" he demanded. "You were supposed to be here around noon. Okay, okay. You'll explain when you get here. How long?"

Eli wrinkled his nose as if the reception was lousy. "Okay, I'll tell Jerry your boys will be ready for a big meal. What? He might have to postpone it? Okay, okay. See you when you get here."

"What's wrong?" Marissa asked, keeping an eye on Jordan but her attention on Eli.

"I'm not sure exactly. He said he'll explain when he gets here. I have a feeling something didn't go right. He said he's okay," Eli added. "But I don't know what that means."

Neither did Marissa. *Okay* could mean anything from he needed ice on his knee to he'd need an appointment with his orthopedist the next day.

She worried, and then she worried some more, all the while preparing a meal for her, Jordan, Eli and Ty that she didn't know if anybody would eat. She kept it simple, lots of macaroni and cheese in the slow cooker, a veggie tray with a ranch dip. She grabbed a bag of potato chips from the cupboard and placed a batch of cookies on a tray, covering them with plastic wrap.

She glanced around at the Christmas decorations, the Nativity set on a corner table, the angel on the mantel, the Christmas tree.

What if Ty had gotten hurt? What if—

Clint came to the back door and called inside. "They're back. I can see them on the hill."

She had about ten minutes to compose herself. Ten minutes to pretend she hadn't been worried every day since Ty had been gone. Ten minutes until she gave him a kiss he wouldn't soon forget.

Ty was concerned for his guests, glad he'd taken his lawyer's advice about liability insurance and wide range coverage. Horses and greenhorns didn't always go together.

He got Brad settled in the truck, excusing himself for a few moments to stop in at the house. He had to see Marissa. Even with the makeshift sling on his arm, Brad didn't seem out of sorts as he regaled Clint with anecdotes about their trip.

Ty mounted the steps to the kitchen and went inside. Marissa was feeding Jordan supper. He went straight to her, took her in his arms and gave her a resounding kiss.

She kissed him back as if she'd missed him, too. After he broke away, she asked, "How are you?"

"I'm fine. I don't have time to talk now. Brad took a spill and I need to get him to the urgent care center and have that arm x-rayed. I don't want him flying out of here with anything wrong with him."

"But you're okay?"

"I'm good. I paced myself as well as them. We took

breaks to see the scenery and hike. They liked the campfires and talked my ear off. This is going to work, Marissa—it really is."

He could tell she wanted to ask about his leg so he answered her before she had to ask. "I'm sore. I need ice. But there will be plenty of time for taking care of it after everybody leaves."

He lifted the lid on the slow cooker and took a whiff. Then he winked at Eli. "Don't you eat it all till I get back."

"Wouldn't think of it," his uncle said with a ghost of a smile.

Ty knew he needed a shower and couldn't wait to get one. But Brad was his responsibility and he was going to accompany him to the urgent care center.

Still, crossing to Jordan, Ty looked him straight in the eye. "Have you been a good boy for your mom?"

"The best," she answered lightly.

Ty kissed his son's forehead, nodded and said, "I'll see you later." He went outside again, the fatigue from the past two days just dropping away.

Two hours later, Ty was back at the Cozy C and Brad was getting some leftovers at his cabin.

No broken bones, thank goodness. His guest had to keep his arm in a sling for a couple of days but flying back home tomorrow wouldn't be a problem. After Ty bid his guests good-night, he returned to the house, eager for supper, that shower and a night with Marissa in his bed.

However, when he got to the kitchen, Marissa's expression was as serious as it had been earlier before he'd explained he'd physically handled the camping trip.

From the monitor, Ty could see Jordan was in bed so he knew there couldn't be a problem with his son. Eli was nowhere in sight, so he must have turned in.

"Ready for supper?" she asked, faking a smile.

He took off his hat and put it on the rack. "I should get a shower."

"You might want to make a phone call first."

There was a note in her voice that alerted him that that's what her expression was all about. "What phone call?"

She nodded to a notepad on the counter. "I took down the information. That man you talked to at the horse auction called."

"Mr. Carrington called?" And as soon as he asked, he began to suspect what this might be about.

"He said he called your cell phone but it went to voice mail."

"I didn't have a signal out there. And I haven't had a chance to check my calls since I got back."

"You might want to check your email, too," she suggested in a flat, even voice. "He has this great job lined up for you as a rodeo promoter. He said he emailed you the particulars. But you need to give him a call. He needs your decision by the new year."

That gave him two weeks to decide. Decide? There was nothing to decide, was there? Still, he knew he should look over the information. He knew he should consider all of his options.

Marissa was studying him intently. "You're going to call him, aren't you?"

"It would be the polite thing to do."

"You're also thinking it might be easier than taking

vacation guests on trail rides and worrying about them getting hurt."

He didn't want to feel defensive about this, but he did. He tried to keep his own tone even. "This isn't about *easier*, Marissa, it's about the best life for everybody. Donaldson's offer is nothing to sneeze at. Unc could be comfortable till the end of his years, and if I had a job with a good income—" He stopped abruptly. Thinking out loud wasn't a good thing around Marissa. He shrugged. "I need to think about all of it carefully."

"But if you took the job as a rodeo promoter, that would mean you'd have to travel, wouldn't it?"

"I haven't talked to Carrington yet. I don't know what's involved. But I suppose it might."

"I thought you wanted to be an everyday dad. I thought you wanted to be around for all of it."

"I do. But I have to be practical, too."

He could see her face fall, and maybe it was more than her expression that fell. Maybe it was her hopes.

"Look, I'm not going to make any decisions tonight," he assured her. "I'm going to call him back, then I'm going to get some supper and a shower. Afterward…" He eyed her with a bit of expectation. "I'd like you to come to my room to sleep tonight."

She turned away from him and pretended to be busy doing something at the counter, but she was really only shifting things around, making up things to do.

"That might not be such a good idea," she admitted, turning to look at him again.

"Because I'm returning his phone call?"

"It's not just that, Ty. You're interested. You might be giving this all up." She motioned to the house and to the broader aspect of the ranch. "To travel from place to place again."

"Let's not discuss this until I know what I'm dealing with."

"Fine. Go make your call. I'll check on Jordan."

And with that, she left the kitchen, leaving Ty wondering how everything had gone to hell in a handbasket so darn fast.

The following day, *upset* didn't begin to describe Marissa's state of mind. She had been dreaming of a future with Ty, and Ty was thinking about leaving again.

Maybe that's why when Scott Donaldson called her at the winery and asked for a meeting in his office, she didn't think twice about it. In fact, she was hopeful he was going to tell her he had more recommendations for her. She could start socking away money for that new apartment and tell Ty she didn't need his child support.

She wasn't going to be stupid. She was going to return to her previous outlook on life—that it was best if she needed no one and depended on no man. She'd begun to depend on Ty, and that had been a mistake.

She left work a little early because she'd told Jase about the appointment and he'd encouraged her to go. He was the best boss.

At the end of the day, she was always eager to pick up Jordan, see his happy little face and hug him in her arms. So this meeting with Scott would be quick.

The developer's office was located on the edge of the town in one of the newer Fawn Grove buildings. It was three stories and housed lawyers, insurance agents and other professional offices. He'd told her he was on the first floor and she easily found his suite. When she stepped into the reception area, she felt encased in luxury—burgundy leather, light gray walls, plush gray carpeting. She was about to approach the receptionist seated at a dark wooden desk when Scott himself emerged from a hall beyond.

He smiled at her and beckoned to her. "Right on time."

"I try to be."

She followed him down the hall, aware of his height, almost the same as Ty's, and the scent of his cologne. But she didn't particularly like cologne on men. She preferred shaving soap and aftershave and the smell of pine and hard work. She shook those thoughts away because they brought a picture of Ty front and center in her mind.

When Scott showed her into his office, he motioned to a pewter-gray leather sofa rather than the chairs in front of his desk. As she sat, he went to the desk, took something from the drawer and brought it with him as he lowered himself beside her.

A little too close, she thought, tempted to move away but thinking that would look rude.

"Do you have another event you want me to plan?" she asked brightly, intending to keep this meeting on a purely business footing.

"I certainly do. After Christmas. It's a groundbreaking event. But we'll have plenty of time because it's at the end of January."

"We'll still need those weeks for preparation," she remarked, wondering about the box with the little bow that he held in his hand.

"We can worry about that after the new year, as well

as the friend or two who asked me about you. They were impressed with my open house."

"Wonderful," she said.

"I have something else I want to talk to you about now."

The wary feeling that had slipped up her spine the moment she'd stepped into his office became more intense. "What would that be?"

"I have something for you." He leaned a little closer and handed her the box.

When she turned questioning eyes on him, he gave a shrug. "Just a token of my appreciation, plus a little Christmas thrown in."

She was tempted just to hand him back the box, tell him she couldn't accept a gift and leave, forgetting about his contacts and possible lucrative events. But what if something silly was in the box? Like a Santa pin with a light-up nose, or something equally benign.

Swallowing hard, she removed the lid with the bow attached and stared at a beautiful silver bangle bracelet.

Trying to keep her wits about her, she said, "It's beautiful, Scott, but I can't accept this." She tried to hand it back to him.

But his hand covered hers. "Put it on and I bet you won't want to take it off."

She was already shaking her head. "No, I can't do that. I—"

Before she could get out another sentence, he started to lean toward her for a kiss.

Oh, no, that was not happening! She wouldn't set herself up in a situation that could only be damaging to everything she held dear.

She quickly stood, still shaking her head. "Scott, I'm

sorry, but I'm involved with Ty Conroy." At least that much was true, even though that involvement might soon be ending. Her heart broke at the thought.

"You said staying there was only temporary." He sounded annoyed, as if he was used to getting his way, and this wasn't the way he'd envisioned this meeting going.

"Our situation is complicated, but I have deep feelings for Ty. He's Jordan's father, and I… Well—"

She certainly wasn't going to explain what was going on and what might happen next. She set the box with the bracelet on the sofa beside him.

Scott stood and started to approach her. She was shaking her head again.

"If we can't have a strictly business relationship, we won't be able to do business. That's the bottom line for me," she said firmly.

With that, she left his office as quickly as she could. When she reached the reception area and realized he hadn't come after her, she breathed a sigh of relief. If she wanted to start an event planning business, she'd have to do it without Scott Donaldson.

Ty hadn't been in the best of moods before physical therapy. He could still see the hurt in Marissa's eyes, and he felt the weight of her disappointment on his shoulders. Yet, what the physical therapist had just told him had to count, too.

"You came through the trail ride fairly well," she'd said.

Fairly well, he thought, and responded, "When I overuse the muscles, it's going to take a few days for them to settle down."

"Yes," she'd agreed, though he hadn't wanted her to. "This is your life now, Mr. Conroy, and I don't know how far you're going to progress from this point. If you do your exercises and don't abuse your knee, it will work well for you. Think about how far you've come, from surgery and a walker and crutches to going on a three-day trail ride. But you must find a balance to handle pain, wear and tear on your knee, and what you want to deal with for the rest of your life."

Find a balance, he thought with annoyance. Just what was that supposed to mean? Only ride a horse one day a week? Not take vacationers out on a trail ride? Or take a different job altogether? Let his uncle retire in style? Live in a condo in town? See Marissa and Jordan whenever he wasn't traveling?

Deep in thought about the launch of the Cozy C as a vacation ranch, living with Marissa and making decisions that would affect them all led him to stop at the sports bar at the edge of town. The Black Boot might have a jukebox filled with country tunes, but the owner also boasted about its several flat-screen TVs streaming the latest sports. Ty could either drive around for a while and think, or he could have a beer and think. Today he chose the beer.

At barely five o'clock, the week before Christmas, the Black Boot wasn't that busy. He was glad of that. Though he might want a little white noise around him, he didn't want to be bombarded with people.

When he stepped inside, he decided to forgo a table and chose a stool at the long wooden bar. However, after he took a seat, he spotted Scott Donaldson's face in the mirror behind the bar. The old-fashioned glass in front of him probably held one of those whiskeys he enjoyed. Expensive whiskeys, Ty corrected in his head.

The bartender came over to Ty immediately, and Ty ordered a beer on draft, fully intending to ignore the real estate developer.

But spotting Ty now, Donaldson made ignoring him out of the question. Sliding the drink down the bar, the developer took the stool next to Ty.

"Good to see you, Conroy," Donaldson said. "I was just thinking about you and your uncle and that pretty woman you have living there with you."

Ty took a slug of his beer and wiped his mouth with the back of his hand. "You're wasting your time thinking about us." If Eli really did want to sell the ranch, maybe they could get an even better price from somebody *other* than this man.

"My offer's the best one you're going to get. I heard you already had a mishap with one of your guests. Those insurance premiums will go up each time you do."

"You let me worry about that. It's really none of your business."

"Maybe, maybe not. But I just had a meeting with Marissa. She and I are going to be working on lots of projects in the new year. And just like your uncle, I'll wear her down."

"Wear her down?" Ty asked, needing to understand the message Donaldson was trying to give him. When he looked into the man's eyes, he saw that the whiskey in front of him hadn't been his first. Was liquor fueling his words?

"Yeah, wear her down. Eventually she's going to agree to go out with me."

Ty wanted to say, *Never! That's not going to happen.* He wanted to say, *She's mine. Don't even look at her.* He wanted to say, *Keep far away from Marissa.* Instead, he said, casually, "I doubt if that will happen."

"Because she's *in-volved.*" Donaldson drew out the word, then added, "With you? Because you're the father of her son? Let's face it, Conroy, I'm a better man than you'll ever be. You'll never have polish. More than that, you'll never be the cowboy you once were. A fake knee? How long is that going to last on a ranch?"

Ty's fist itched to connect with Donaldson's jaw. He'd been a wrestler, after all, and he was in better shape now than he'd ever been in his life, fake knee or not. He could wrap Donaldson in a choke hold that would make him take back his words.

But in the end, what good would that do? In the end, he'd still be in the same predicament he was in now.

Ty stood and took a bill from his pocket. He placed it on the counter and gave a nod to the bartender, saying, "Keep the change."

As he walked away, Donaldson called after him, "The Cozy C is a whole lot of work you don't need. Sell it and start a new life. Unless you don't know how to be anything but a cowboy."

Minutes later, after climbing into his truck and starting it up, Ty drove back to the ranch, Donaldson's words ringing in his ears.

On the drive to the ranch, he debated asking Marissa about her meeting with Donaldson. Or should he not say anything and see if *she* did? Would she keep their meeting a secret?

Like she kept Jordan's birth a secret? a little voice in his head asked.

When he entered the house, he didn't see Marissa. This time of day, she usually was in the kitchen preparing supper.

Ty noticed Eli in the living room watching TV. He went to his uncle, but before he could even ask, Eli said, "She's upstairs with Jordan."

"Is something wrong?" Ty asked.

"I'm not sure," Eli responded.

Ty was determined to find out what that meant. Mounting the stairs, he found Marissa exiting Jordan's room. She partially closed the door. He could feel the tension between them as soon as their gazes met. Everything she'd said, everything he'd said, whirled about them like disturbing static.

"How was physical therapy?" she asked.

"I'm finished with it. There's not much more I can accomplish there that I can't do on my own. What's going on with Jordan? He never takes a nap this time of day."

"He didn't nap at all today at day care, and he has the sniffles. He ate a little bit for me. I really don't know what to do about tomorrow. I don't want to send him to day care with a cold. Jase and I are supposed to have a meeting with an influential distributor. But I guess I'll call him and ask for a personal day. Maybe he can postpone the meeting," she said, almost to herself.

"Don't call Jase. I'll take care of Jordan tomorrow. I have to do end-of-the-year bookwork and update our social media sites."

"If he has a cold, he could be cranky. You might not get anything done."

"If I don't get anything done that doesn't matter. He's my son."

Marissa looked as if she wanted to say something to that, maybe all the reasons why he shouldn't consider the rodeo promoting job, but she didn't. Rather she said, "If you change your mind, I can call Jase in the morning."

Her words annoyed him. "I won't change my mind."

When she would have slipped by him down the stairs, he decided not to play games or keep any secrets. "I ran into your friend Donaldson at the Black Boot."

Her eyes widened a little. "My *friend*?" She emphasized the word as if challenging him to dispute it.

"Whatever he is," Ty conceded. "He said you two had a meeting."

Now her eyes looked troubled. She looked away for a second. What was that about?

But then she returned his steady gaze. "He wanted to give me a thank-you gift—a Christmas present. But I refused it."

"What was it?" Ty asked. He had ordered Marissa a handcrafted leather purse that should be ready tomorrow. He was curious about what Donaldson had come up with.

"It was a bracelet."

"Something you'd wear?" Ty asked, wondering what it looked like.

"I didn't accept it, Ty. Scott is…" She stopped. "Scott *was* a business associate."

"Was?" He felt as if he was playing twenty questions. Why didn't she just come out with what had happened?

"It doesn't matter. I just don't think I'll be planning any more parties for him."

"Did he make a pass at you? Did you kiss him?"

At first, hurt flashed in Marissa's dark brown eyes.

Then it was quickly followed by spirited anger. "You're never going to trust me, are you? You're never even going to try to forget that I didn't tell you about Jordan. Maybe that's why you're thinking about taking this promoting job. Then you won't have to deal with us, the relationship between us and what we do or don't have. Trust is as much a decision as it is a feeling, Ty. If we don't have trust, we have nothing." She waved her arms and turned away. "I've got to get supper on."

He caught her elbow before she could walk away. "Do *you* trust *me*?"

She looked at him. Her answer was quick in coming. "How can I when I don't know what you're committed to? How can I when you think being a sometimes dad is going to be enough?"

With that, she yanked away and hurried down the stairs.

Ty was glad he had Jordan to focus on tomorrow, because thinking about Marissa just made his heart hurt.

Chapter Thirteen

Ty was in a panic.

When Marissa had left this morning, Jordan's head was stuffy, but he hadn't had the cough that had developed throughout the morning and the fever that had spiked just now. Should he try to get the fever down? If he did that, what about the cough? Should he just walk Jordan around, hoping he'd nap, hoping it didn't get worse? Eli wasn't around to give his two cents. He'd gone into town for a dental appointment and then he was going to play checkers with friends at the feed store.

Ty's patience had just about run out on all levels. Waiting to see if his son's cough worsened didn't seem to be a good parenting strategy. But what did he know? He'd only been doing this for a little over a month.

He dialed Marissa's cell, but his call went to voice mail. He didn't leave a message because he wasn't done trying to contact her. He dialed the winery, but he was prompted to leave a voice message there, too. Then he remembered, Marissa and Jase had a meeting with a new distributor. Ty didn't have the company name. He'd been upset with Marissa, upset with himself, upset about the situation and he hadn't covered the bases.

But he did have a fallback plan. Kaitlyn Preston's practice and cell number were on the refrigerator. Call the practice or call the pediatrician's cell?

Call her cell.

Jordan was crying softly now, and Ty jiggled him as he walked.

Kaitlyn picked up.

"It's Ty Conroy," he said quickly. "I can't reach Marissa and Jordan's sick, fever of one hundred and one, and a cough, stuffy nose, too. What do I do?"

"You said a cough?" she asked calmly.

"Yes, it came on fast. He didn't have it this morning."

"Bring him to my office. Do you have the address?"

That was on the card on the refrigerator, too. "I do. I'll see you in ten minutes."

Ty knew he had to stay as calm as he could. He had to bundle Jordan up in the damp weather. He had to drive like a sensible cowboy rather than a reckless one.

And he did.

Kaitlyn ushered them back to an exam room, thoroughly examined Jordan, then looked at Ty with concerned eyes.

"I'm going to admit him for observation. He has bronchitis."

"Admit him?" For a moment, the words wouldn't sink in.

"To the hospital in Sacramento. I'm finished with

appointments here for the day. I was just following up on patient charts. Are you okay driving him there?"

"Sure, I am," Ty said, knowing his GPS would find the hospital just fine. It's a shame it couldn't direct the rest of his life.

"I'll meet you there," Kaitlyn said.

Ty got Jordan dressed, scared to his boot heels for his son, knowing he had to leave a message for Marissa to tell her what was happening.

An hour and a half later, dealing with enough red tape to strangle a moose, Ty sat beside his son's crib, watching fluid and medication flow from the IV bag into his little body. Ty hoped and prayed Marissa would get his message soon and understand what was happening.

As he sat there, studying Jordan's little face—a combination of his face and Marissa's—as he brushed his fingers over the little boy's dark brown hair, his warm skin, his flushed cheeks, Ty knew what was more important than anything else in this world. His son—and Marissa.

As he sat there, finally comprehending the magnitude of decisions parents had to make for their children, he understood why Marissa hadn't told him about her pregnancy. She'd had to make decisions, for herself and for her unborn baby, that were the best she knew how to make. Coming from a broken family, a father who hadn't loved her, a mother who had struggled to make ends meet, she'd wanted better for her son. She'd wanted stability and love and a support group that would last. She'd dismissed the idea of a dad who was a traveling cowboy because that hadn't fit in with the best plan for Jordan.

He got that now. It had been nothing against him. She'd understood who he was and what he'd wanted. And that hadn't seemed to be roots.

She was afraid he wouldn't choose roots now.

Sometimes what looked good on paper didn't pan out in reality.

The reality was—he loved Marissa. He loved her up and down, sideways and backward. She wasn't simply his son's mom, she was the love of Ty's life. He should have recognized that fact in the way he liked being with her, the way she made him smile just by coming into a room and the way he felt like a better person just by being with her. Oh, he'd relegated all of it to sex and desire and the physical satisfaction they found with each other. There was no denying that. But there was so much more, and he knew she felt it, too.

At least he hoped she felt it, too. He hoped she wanted more than a father for Jordan. He hoped she wanted a husband for a lifetime.

Marissa had never been this afraid before—not ever. She'd tried to return Ty's call. But in certain parts of the hospital, cell phones had to be turned off. Apparently the pediatrics unit was one of them. She'd tried anyway to tell him she was coming, to ask him a hundred and one questions, to be reassured that their son would be okay. But his voice mail had directed her to leave a message. She'd simply said, "I'm coming."

Her baby was in a hospital. Her anxiety made swallowing difficult.

When she arrived at the desk in pediatrics, Kaitlyn was there talking to a nurse. Her friend spotted her, placed a chart back in its rack and came forward, enveloping her in a hug.

Marissa blinked back tears. She couldn't cry now. She had to be strong. "Where's Jordan?" she asked with a catch in her voice.

"Ty's with him. I'll take you to him."

"I don't understand what happened. He wasn't that sick when I left this morning. I never would have gone. I never *should* have gone."

"Ty acted when he should have. That's what's important. Jordan has bronchitis, but we'll get it turned around."

At the door to Jordan's room, Marissa was overcome by the sight of her baby hooked up to an IV and monitors. She rushed to him, mindful that Ty was at the crib's side, looking worried.

Ty didn't hesitate to wrap his arm around her shoulders as she bent to kiss her son. Ty's low voice rumbled in her ear. "His fever's down a bit, just in the past half hour. He's been on fluids and antibiotics. It's going to be okay, Marissa. I know it is."

Marissa turned to look at Ty then, and when she did, she knew she loved him with every inch of her heart. She'd been wrong not to tell him when she'd gotten pregnant. She'd been wrong to assume he wouldn't know the first thing about being a dad, or that he couldn't be committed because her own father had left. Because Ty was a rodeo cowboy, she'd jumped to the conclusion he wouldn't care about his son. She'd been so wrong about that, too. He was a great dad, and whether he took the promoter's job or he stayed on the Cozy C, she *loved* him.

She had to tell him that, but she couldn't do it now

when they were both so worried. She couldn't do it now when he might think she just needed his support. Somehow she had to convince him that she could be the wife he needed, no matter what he chose to do.

He pushed his chair over behind her so she could sit by Jordan's side. Then he found another and they waited together.

It was midnight when Ty tapped Marissa's hand. They were seated in recliners the hospital staff had wheeled in so they could sleep in the room with Jordan.

"Are you awake?" he asked.

Yes, she was awake. Too many thoughts circled in a continuous loop in her head for her to sleep. Ty stood, took her hand and pulled her up out of the chair. A dim light shone over Jordan's bed. A low murmur of voices, muffled footsteps and lowered lighting crept in the partially open door.

"I can't wait any longer to tell you something," Ty began.

Marissa's heart started racing. Maybe she should stop him. Maybe she should tell him what she had to say first. "I have something to tell you, too."

In the shadowed room, she saw him frown. "I know ladies are supposed to go first, but I've got to say this. I've come to some decisions sitting here by Jordan's bedside. First of all, I've got to explain something. For the past several months I thought I'd lost almost everything—my ability to be physically whole, my rodeo career, a kind of life that used to matter to me. But none of that makes any sense anymore, or comes even close to what I feel for you and Jordan. Today I learned what really matters—our son and our strength as a couple. I love you, Marissa. I think I've loved you since high school. For sure, I've loved you since that night after the wedding when we made love. I know it's a lot to take in right now, but I need to know. Will you marry me? Will you help me make the Cozy C a success? Will you give me your heart for a lifetime?"

She could hardly believe what she was hearing. She could hardly believe her dreams were going to come true.

"You want to marry me?"

"Yes, I do. I love you. I want more babies, and I want to give them the legacy of the Cozy C and the possibility of it lasting far beyond our children having *their* kids."

She flung her arms around his neck and held him so tight she wasn't sure either of them could breathe. "Yes, I'll marry you. I wanted to tell you how much I love you and that I'd be by your side whether you wanted to be a rodeo promoter or head up a vacation ranch. It doesn't matter to me anymore, Ty. My home and Jordan's are with you, wherever you go, whatever you do. I don't want you to ever doubt that."

"It seems we've both been doing a lot of thinking," he said in a husky voice.

"And feeling," she assured him in a whisper just before his lips came down on hers.

This was going to be a Christmas she'd never forget, and one she and Ty would tell their son about for years to come.

Epilogue

Christmas Eve

Marissa's heart melted as Jordan sat on Ty's knee while he read the Christmas story. Jase and Sara's little girl, Amy, sat cross-legged on the floor at Ty's feet, staring up at him with wide eyes. Adam and Kaitlyn had invited everyone into their home for a Christmas Eve celebration. Somehow Ty had ended up with the Bible and reading about what had happened when a star brighter than any other had graced the sky.

Marissa sent up a prayer of gratitude that their little boy was so resilient. He'd come home from the hospital the day after he'd been admitted. Though he was still taking antibiotics, he was his happy, energetic little self. At the moment, though, he was entranced by Ty's voice, if not the words.

As Marissa scanned the room, she noticed Kaitlyn

beaming, pregnant and expectant. She and Adam were happy in their new home and couldn't wait for their child to arrive. Adam's sister Tina had been invited, too, and she sat in one of the armchairs, happily cradling her little girl, who was fast asleep. As Marissa watched Jase and Sara exchange looks, she had the feeling it wouldn't be long until Sara announced they were having a baby, too.

Eli sat in a rocker on the other side of the fireplace, watching his nephew and grand-nephew, taking in friends and family that had expanded his life. Hannah stood beside him, her hand on his shoulder. This was their official first date.

As Ty finished reading, he closed the leather-bound book. The fire in the fireplace popped as Jordan squiggled, wanting to be let down. He saw an opportunity to explore with all of the people around him he liked best.

Sara and Kaitlyn were on their feet now, ready to uncover the food on the table and pull more from the refrigerator and counter. Marissa was about to help them when Ty clapped his hands for everyone's attention.

"I have an announcement to make."

Everyone looked his way. He opened his arm to Marissa and she went to join him.

"Marissa and I have set the date. We're going to be married the last Saturday in January, and we want all of you to be there. We put it off for a few weeks because I wanted Marissa to be able to plan the wedding she always wanted."

That's exactly what Ty had told her, and she had already started ordering flowers, looking online at dresses, choosing one with a Western flair. She was so excited and she knew her happiness showed. So did Ty's.

"And there will be a reception afterward at the church social hall that I'm taking care of," Eli announced. "You see, I sold off a few acres of the Cozy C so some other folks can have a grand vista, too."

That had been a decision Eli had made easily, and Ty had encouraged. An offer from a developer in Sacramento had given Eli the cash to pay for the reception and more importantly a nest egg for his future, as well as the confidence that he needed to finally enter into a relationship with Hannah.

So much had happened in such a short time, but Marissa felt it all was just right.

After everyone had congratulated them with hugs and kisses and assured the couple they'd be at the wedding, Ty asked Sara, "Can you watch Jordan for a few minutes?"

"Of course I can," she answered with a bright smile.

"We won't be long," he told her as he took Marissa's hand and led her to the front door.

After they stepped outside, Marissa asked, "What are we doing? The Christmas celebration's in there."

"I want to give you a special Christmas present now."

"We have all night," she teased.

He chuckled. "Yes, we do, and days and nights after that. We were so busy this afternoon—I didn't want to rush this."

"Rush what?" He'd already asked her to marry him. What more did he have to say?

Taking a box from his pocket, he held it in the palm of his hand. "We have good luck coming. I can feel it. We're booked solid the first two weeks in January, and already guests are calling about February and March."

"The Cozy C is going to be the best vacation ranch in the country," she said with confidence.

"In a year, we might even be able to add a cabin or two," Ty said.

Now she studied him carefully. "I know all this."

"Good." He took the lid from the little box and showed her what was inside. It was a Princess-cut diamond that sparkled under the porch light.

"It's beautiful!" she breathed. "Will you put it on for me?"

Ty took the diamond from the box and slipped it onto her finger. It fit perfectly.

He wrapped his arms around her and brought her close. "I can't wait for you to be my wife," he murmured, right before he kissed her.

Marissa's head swam as it always did when he kissed her. She gave and took as he did. When they finally broke apart, she whispered, "I love you, Ty Conroy."

He smoothed her hair away from her face. "I love you, too, Marissa Lopez soon-to-be Conroy."

She glanced at the ring again as if she couldn't believe it was there. Then she gazed up at the sky. "It's as bright as any one of those stars."

Ty pointed to a star in the east. "It's like that one, a little brighter than all the rest."

When he kissed her again, Marissa knew their love would last a lifetime and beyond. She'd found her happily-ever-after with Ty. Her forever cowboy. Her husband to be. Her love for a lifetime.

* * * * *

Available August 18, 2015

#2425 An Officer and a Maverick
Montana Mavericks: What Happened at the Wedding?
by Teresa Southwick
Lani Dalton needs to distract on-duty Officer Russ Campbell from her rowdy brother.
Instead, they wind up locked in a cell together, where sparks ignite. Russ isn't eager
to trust another woman after he had his heart stomped on once before...but the
deputy might just lasso this darling Dalton for good!

#2426 The Bachelor Takes a Bride
Those Engaging Garretts!
by Brenda Harlen
Marco Palermo believes in love at first sight—now, if only he could get Jordyn Garrett
to agree with him! A wager leads to a date and a sizzling kiss, but can Marco open
Jordyn up to love and make her his forever?

#2427 Destined to Be a Dad
Welcome to Destiny
by Christyne Butler
Liam Murphy just discovered he's a daddy—fifteen years too late. The cowboy is
taken with his daughter and her mother, Missy Dobbs. The beautiful Brit was the
one who got away, but Liam knows Destiny, Wyoming, is where he and his girls are
meant to be together.

#2428 A Sweetheart for the Single Dad
The Camdens of Colorado
by Victoria Pade
Tender-hearted Lindie Camden is making up for her family's misdeeds by helping
out the Camdens' archrival, Sawyer Huffman, on a community project. Sawyer's
good heart and even better looks soon have her dreaming of happily-ever-after
with the sexy single dad...

#2429 Coming Home to a Cowboy
Family Renewal
by Sheri WhiteFeather
Horse trainer Kade Quinn heads to Montana after uncovering his long-lost son. But
he remains wary of the child's mother, Bridget Wells. She once lit his body and heart
on fire, and time hasn't dulled their passion for each other—and their family!

#2430 The Rancher's Surprise Son
Gold Buckle Cowboys
by Christine Wenger
Cowboy Cody Masters has only ever loved one woman—Laura, the beautiful
daughter of his arrogant neighbor. So when he finds out that Laura had their
child, he's shocked. Can Cody reclaim what's his and build the family he's always
dreamed of with Laura and their son?

**YOU CAN FIND MORE INFORMATION ON UPCOMING HARLEQUIN® TITLES,
FREE EXCERPTS AND MORE AT WWW.HARLEQUIN.COM.**

HSECNM0815

REQUEST YOUR FREE BOOKS!
2 FREE NOVELS PLUS 2 FREE GIFTS!

HARLEQUIN®

SPECIAL EDITION
Life, Love & Family

Marco Palermo is convinced Jordyn Garrett is The One for him. But it'll be a challenge to convince the beautiful brunette to open her heart to him—and the happily-ever-after only he can give her!

Read on for a sneak preview of
THE BACHELOR TAKES A BRIDE, *the latest book in*
Brenda Harlen's *popular miniseries,*
THOSE ENGAGING GARRETTS!:
THE CAROLINA COUSINS.

He settled his hands lightly on her hips, holding her close but not too tight. He wanted her to know that this was her choice while leaving her in no doubt about what he wanted. She pressed closer to him, and the sensation of her soft curves against his body made him ache.

He parted her lips with his tongue and she opened willingly. She tasted warm and sweet—with a hint of vanilla from the coffee she'd drank—and the exquisite flavor of her spread through his blood, through his body, like an addictive drug.

He felt something bump against his shin. Once. Twice.

The cat, he realized, in the same moment he decided he didn't dare ignore its warning.

Not that he was afraid of Gryffindor, but he was afraid of scaring off Jordyn. Beneath her passionate response, he sensed a lingering wariness and uncertainty.

Slowly, reluctantly, he eased his lips from hers.

She drew in an unsteady breath, confusion swirling in her deep green eyes when she looked at him. "What… what just happened here?"

"I think we just confirmed that there's some serious chemistry between us."

She shook her head. "I'm not going to go out with you, Marco."

There was a note of something—almost like panic—in her voice that urged him to proceed cautiously. "I don't mind staying in," he said lightly.

She choked on a laugh. "I'm not going to have sex with you, either."

"Not tonight," he agreed. "I'm not *that* easy."

This time, she didn't quite manage to hold back the laugh, though sadness lingered in her eyes.

"You have a great laugh," he told her.

Her gaze dropped and her smile faded. "I haven't had much to laugh about in a while."

"Are you ever going to tell me about it?"

He braced himself for one of her flippant replies, a deliberate brush-off, and was surprised by her response.

"Maybe," she finally said. "But not tonight."

It was an acknowledgment that she would see him again, and that was enough for now.

Don't miss
THE BACHELOR TAKES A BRIDE
by Brenda Harlen,
available September 2015 wherever
Harlequin® Special Edition books and ebooks are sold.

www.Harlequin.com

HSEEXP0815

THE WORLD IS BETTER WITH

Romance

Harlequin has everything from contemporary, passionate and heartwarming to suspenseful and inspirational stories.

Whatever your mood, we have a romance just for you!